# Married for Christmas

## NOELLE ADAMS

This book is a work of fiction. Names, characters, places, and incidents are the product of the author's imagination or are used fictitiously. Any resemblance to actual events, locales, or persons, living or dead, is coincidental.

Copyright © 2013 by Noelle Adams. All rights reserved, including the right to reproduce, distribute, or transmit in any form or by any means.

# AUTHOR'S NOTE

The hero of this book is a pastor, but this is not an inspirational romance. It's a regular contemporary romance featuring characters who happen to be religious. Spirituality is an important aspect of human experience and the lives of a lot of people, but it's often surprisingly absent from contemporary romances. Because of that, I thought I'd write this note to prepare readers of this book. The point of this story is not to present any sort of religious message, but because faith is important to these characters, the plot and their development turns on their spiritual condition as much as anything else. In writing a story like this, the challenge is that there's likely to be too much religion for some readers and too little for others. I don't know if I navigated this difficult creative challenge successfully, but I do believe it's worth the attempt.

# ONE

Jessica Cameron had to propose marriage in a couple of hours, and she was a little nervous about it.

Trying to keep the anxiety at bay, she focused on the three computer monitors on her desk, trying to wrap up the day's work before she headed over to Daniel's. Focus was one thing she'd always done well. She'd been working as a web developer for seven years—three of those years working from home—and she'd never had any problem avoiding distractions.

Today was different, however.

It wasn't every day a woman popped the question to one of her best friends.

As it happened, an impromptu conference call with her team took up the last hour of her workday, saving her from endless minutes of pretending to accomplish something constructive. When it was over, she loaded her dog, Bear, into the car, stopped at a Thai place for takeout, and then drove over to Daniel's.

Only after she left did she realize she should have worked harder on her appearance. She'd changed out of the sweats she normally wore at home, but she'd just put on jeans and a sweatshirt, with her hair pulled into a low ponytail and no makeup.

She looked the way she always looked—average, forgettable, no frills.

Daniel wasn't likely to be awed by her appearance even if she'd made an effort, so she decided it didn't really matter.

He stood just outside the side door of his bungalow as she pulled into the driveway. She tried not to notice how adorably rumpled he looked in his khakis, wrinkled dress shirt, and disarrayed hair. He had dark eyes and a fit, athletic body, and he didn't shave often enough, so he always had something between stubble and a short beard.

After he'd graduated from seminary six years ago, Daniel had gotten a job as pastor of a small church in the Charlotte area where she'd been living since college. She'd known him all her life, and his handsome face was as familiar to her as her own.

She never imagined she'd be proposing marriage to him, although she'd daydreamed often enough about him proposing to her.

He was frowning as he walked over to open the driver-side door of her car. She beat him to it, climbing out as he approached.

"What's wrong?" she asked, surprised because he normally greeted her with a warm smile.

"Your engine doesn't sound right."

"My engine sounds fine."

"No, it doesn't." He leaned over to pull the hood release in her four-year-old sedan. "Something's wrong. You can't ignore it when something sounds off in your car."

"I'm not ignoring it—wait!"

Daniel had been about to slam the door before she stopped him.

"Bear is coming out," she explained, reaching down to rub the dog's nose, which had almost been smashed by the closing door.

Bear was a Samoyed—big, long-haired, and pure white.

Daniel shook his head. "Why did you bring the dog?"

"Her name is Bear. Not 'the dog.' She wanted to come, so why would I leave her by herself all evening?"

"Because she's a dog. Not a guest at a dinner party."

"She's not going to hurt anything. Don't be grumpy. You've never even tried to get to know her."

Bear wagged her tailed excitedly at Daniel until he deigned to give her a token pat on the head.

He looked tired, she realized, as he pulled open the hood of her car and peered in at the engine. She wasn't sure he always got enough sleep or had regular meals.

"You don't have to mess with my car," she said, adjusting her bag of Thai food to the other hand as she went over to stand beside him. "It's fine."

"It is not fine." He reached in to fiddle with something.

Daniel loved to work on cars and wasted ridiculous amounts of time on his old pickup truck.

Jessica tried not to look at his long legs and firm butt as he leaned over but didn't entirely succeed. To hide her response to how hot he looked, she said sharply, "Stop. You'll get your clothes all greasy."

He glanced down at himself as if surprised he was wearing clothes at all. "They'll wash."

She tugged at his arm. "That's a good shirt, Daniel, and grease isn't easy to get off. Stop messing with my car. If something is wrong with it, I'll take it to a service place."

"Why would you pay someone else to—"

"Because *they'll* know what they're doing."

"I know what I'm doing."

"Maybe, and maybe not. I can't afford for you to play around with my car. Our food is getting cold, so please leave my engine alone."

With a sigh, he slammed the hood closed. He still looked tired as he leaned against the car, but amusement glinted in his eyes. "I don't think you trust me."

"I trust you with theology and with helping me through problems and to always beat me at Scrabble and to be smarter than anyone else and to invariably whine about my dog. I don't trust you with my car." With her free hand, she grabbed his shirt and tried to pull him away from the hood and toward the side door to the house.

He smiled in that way he had that made her heart flip over a couple of times. "I'm good with cars." He resisted her tugging by the simple act of refusing to budge.

"Uh-huh." She got a better grip on his shirt and tugged again, this time pulling so hard she accidentally pulled his shirttail out from his trousers. She gasped in surprise and immediately let go of his shirt, but not before she'd seen a quick glimpse of a very fine abdomen when the fabric was pulled up.

Daniel laughed, either at the mishap or her startled expression.

"Sorry," she mumbled, feeling ridiculously embarrassed, although there was no good reason to feel that way. "Why are you so dressed up today anyway?"

"There was a lunch prayer meeting for local pastors." He straightened up and stuffed his shirt back into his pants, still half chuckling. "Evidently they're still willing to let me into the club."

She frowned at the self-deprecating words. "Don't talk like that. What happened to the church wasn't your fault."

A couple of months ago, the church he'd pastored for the past six years had fallen apart when a young couple in the church filed for divorce. Normally, a divorce wouldn't have such a monumental effect on a congregation, but the couple belonged to the two founding families in the church, and a feud between the families had erupted in the wake of the divorce. Daniel had done his best to pursue reconciliation and bring the congregation back together, but it was a losing battle. Finally both families had left, along with other families who sided with one or the other, and the people who remained weren't enough to sustain the church. Or the salary of its pastor.

He'd never complained. He'd never berated the people involved. But she knew how heartbreaking it had been for him to watch the work of so many years in building a church simply go down the drain.

He sighed. "If you say so."

"I *do* say so." Her heart ached for him, and she put a hand on his chest—the only means she had at her disposal of comforting him. "You couldn't have done anything better than you did. Sometimes those things just happen."

"Yeah," he breathed.

He was gazing at her now with something deep and speaking in his eyes, the laughter transforming into something else. Her breath hitched at the sight of it, and her blood started to throb in response.

She stood there, her hand resting on his chest, waiting for *something*.

Then his face changed, and he took the bag of food out of her hand. "I still think you should let me work on your car."

Jessica felt her heart thud back down to its proper location. She managed to murmur, "Never going to happen," in a casually teasing voice and started for the door, calling for Bear to come although the dog needed no encouragement to follow the food.

They went into his kitchen, which was in the state his house always was—basically clean but cluttered with books, unopened mail, and grocery bags, some with items still in them.

She'd been distracted by the intense moment before, but she suddenly remembered that she had to propose to him in a few minutes. She went cold with a wave of fear and tried to swallow over it.

To focus on something else, she opened the dishwasher and pulled out two clean plates. He never put his clean dishes in the cabinets. Sometimes she did it for him, but usually the clean dishes stayed in the dishwasher until it was empty—then he filled it up again with the dirty ones.

"What's the matter?" he asked, taking little cartons of rice, curry, and seafood out of the bag she'd brought.

"Nothing. What do you mean?"

"You look upset or nervous about something."

"I'm not upset or nervous." It wasn't exactly true, but this was hardly the time to blurt out the marriage proposal. She had it all planned out. After dinner, they would naturally start to talk about his job situation. Then, very smoothly, she would offer her well-reasoned suggestion, exactly as she'd planned it out in her mind as she lay awake all last night.

"Did you talk to your mom today?" Daniel asked, shamelessly pinching a stray piece of shrimp from her carton and putting it in his mouth.

She narrowed her eyes to make sure he knew she'd seen the shrimp snatching. "Yeah. She sounded all right. She knew who I was."

"That's good. So what's the problem?"

"No problem. I told you. I'm just hungry."

"It looks like there's a problem." He didn't look annoyed or displeased. In fact, his brown eyes were still warm and laid-back. But he was always like that—somehow knowing what she was feeling and not leaving it alone until he found out the whole story.

"There's no problem," she said, trying to sound as relaxed as he was.

"You sure?"

Her attempt at staying relaxed failed miserably. "Listen to what I'm telling you. There. Is. Not. A. Problem."

"All right. Fine. Weren't you just complaining that *I* was grumpy? No reason to be in a bad mood about it."

"I'm not in a bad mood." She tried to moderate her tone, but sometimes it was really exasperating that she couldn't hide anything from him. "Why don't you ever believe what I tell you?"

He looked like he was hiding a smile as he picked up the two plates he'd prepared. "Because you don't always tell me the truth." When she opened her mouth to object to this statement, he spoke over her to continue, "Okay, that's an exaggeration. But you don't always tell me the whole story."

"You don't always *need* the whole story," she grumbled, grabbing two bottles of water and following him out to the living room to settle on the couch.

"Well, I *want* the whole story whether I need it or not. So why are you so stubborn about giving it to me?"

"Because some things are none of your business."

He chuckled at her bad-tempered tone, and she couldn't help but smile too. It was nearly impossible to stay annoyed with him for very long. No matter how infuriating he was, he always had her best interests at heart.

Plus he was just so adorable, even when he was being stubborn.

He took a long sip of water and leaned back on the couch, his plate in his lap. He offered brief, silent thanks for the food and then gazed at her with brown eyes that suddenly looked soft.

Her breath hitched at the fond expression.

She'd been going to wait until after they ate, but now might be a good time to work in the marriage proposal.

"Daniel," she began.

Bear had planted herself next to the couch, sitting upright and staring fixedly at the food. After being ignored for longer than she was willing to tolerate, she raised one paw.

"No, you're not getting any food," Daniel told the dog.

"Don't be rude." Jessica frowned at him and then said to Bear, "I'll give you a snack later."

When she turned back, the soft expression and her nerve were both gone.

"But seriously, Jessica," Daniel began after swallowing over another bite, "you don't have to tell me everything if you don't want, but I don't like that you're so isolated."

This shift in tone and the unexpected topic made her stiffen her shoulders. "I'm not isolated. What are you talking about?"

"You work from home. You don't have any family but your mom. You don't hang out with friends much."

"I hang out plenty," she replied, immediately defensive. "I talk to my neighbors. I do things at church whenever I can. I hang out with *you* enough to drive me crazy. You know I did more before my mom... I have to leave every weekend to go see her."

"I know."

"I'm never going to be a social butterfly, but that doesn't mean I'm isolated."

"Okay." He was watching her as he chewed, and he looked concerned, thoughtful, observant.

She wasn't comfortable with any of those things. "I don't need you to be worrying about me."

"Okay." His expression changed, and he gave her a lopsided grin. "I'll remind you of that the next time you worry about *me*."

"Wait. That's different. Of course I'll worry about *you*."

He arched his eyebrows, and she returned the expression with nothing but a cool glare. Eventually, he chuckled and returned to his food.

She ate for a minute too, barely tasting the food although Thai was one of her favorites. As she chewed, she glanced around the comfortable living room. It had been decorated by Lila, Daniel's wife, and he hadn't changed a single thing in the room since she died almost two years ago.

Without conscious volition, Jessica's eye rested on the framed picture of Lila on the console table. The woman in the photo was dark-haired, small, and achingly pretty.

Daniel must have noticed the direction of her gaze because he said, his voice softer, "I know you worried about me after Lila died, but I'm really okay now."

"I know. I think you've done great." Her chest still hurt at the memory of his sweet wife of seven years who'd died far too young in a car accident.

For a couple of months after her death, Daniel had been a wreck. She could barely stand the thought of how torn up he'd been at losing his wife. She wasn't entirely convinced he had healed the way he should have—every once in a while, something he did or said would prompt a thread of worry—but he was definitely better now than he'd been before, and he seemed to have returned to his friendly, considerate, and articulate self.

That line of thought reminded her of her mission this evening. She gulped down some water and tried to recall the details of her plan. In an attempt to get closer to the relevant topic, she asked, "Have you heard anything more from Micah?"

Daniel was already done with his food, so he put his plate on the coffee table. "Yeah. He called again today. He said the pulpit committee wants me, but the Session is still hesitating."

Micah was Daniel's brother who still lived in Willow Park, the town in the mountains of North Carolina where both Jessica and Daniel had grown up. Micah had recently started again attending their hometown church, the church where Daniel had spent the past month candidating to become the pastor.

"It's still because you're not married?"

He gave a half shrug. "Yeah. And because I'm young. But Micah said if I was married, my age wouldn't be such a big deal. I guess I can understand their concerns. It's a traditional, old-fashioned church in a small town. They worry about having a young pastor who isn't married." He gave a rough sigh that was almost a groan. "I just don't want to move to South Dakota."

When his church had fallen apart, he'd had to go back on the job market. Their particular Presbyterian denomination was small though, so empty pulpits weren't easy to come by. He'd done a national search and was a finalist at several churches. He'd gotten one offer from a church in South Dakota but was waiting to hear from Willow Park before he made his decision.

Jessica hated the thought of his moving all the way to South Dakota. She hated the thought so much it made her want to cry. "I know. That would be a rough transition," she said, taking another bite without really tasting it.

He exhaled deeply and dropped his head against the back the couch. "Maybe I'm supposed to be in South Dakota though. I thought it seemed so clear when Willow Park was looking exactly when I was available. I've wanted to be the pastor of First Pres practically my whole life."

"I know you have." Jessica stifled a flutter of fond feeling at the memory of him as a boy. His grandfather had been the pastor of First Presbyterian Church in Willow Park. She remembered after church on Sunday afternoons Daniel would get up behind the pulpit and pretend to preach to her and all her friends. They'd all been awed that he knew so many Bible verses and sounded as dignified as an adult.

"But that just means it's not likely to happen," Daniel murmured, so softly he might have been talking to himself.

Jessica stiffened. "What is *that* supposed to mean?"

He gave a dry laugh, intentionally shrugging off any significance. "Nothing. Just that my dreams don't come true."

It wasn't hard to see why he'd say it, why he'd *think* it. He'd lost his wife. He'd lost his church here. He'd just about lost his chance to pastor the church he'd always wanted. But the words still made her chest clench. "Don't say things like that. Maybe it's not at all like you'd planned, but it's not like God wants you to be unhappy."

He gave another huff of bitter amusement. "Well, he couldn't have designed it better if he'd been trying."

It was just one of those things people said—thoughtless, mostly ironic, not intended to be taken seriously. But Jessica was suddenly afraid that Daniel *did* believe it. She stared at his tired, handsome face—intelligence and self-deprecation visible in his expression. "Daniel?" she asked very softly.

He smiled at her, his natural look, and shook off whatever he'd been brooding about the moment before. "I was joking. Just being stupid. You know I don't mean that."

She was relieved he'd said it although the thread of worry still remained.

"Anyway," Daniel continued, obviously reaching back toward a more normal conversation, "Micah said they're still discussing it. The congregational vote isn't until Sunday. Who knows what God has in mind?"

It was the right time. Exactly the opening she needed. She might as well use it. "Yeah. I've been thinking about that." She took a long, shaky breath and lost her courage before she could get out the rest of her planned words. She set her plate down even though she'd only eaten half her food.

"What do you mean?" He reached over to pick up her plate. "You done?"

"Yeah, go ahead." She watched as he started to finish her food and tried to remember what she needed to say.

"What did you mean?" Daniel prompted.

"I don't know." She couldn't quite get to the marriage proposal yet, so she stalled a little. "I was just thinking about what God might have in mind. For me too, I mean."

"About what?"

"About everything. You and I are kind of the same in some ways. My dreams never come true either. I just feel like I've been in a holding pattern. For years." She hadn't planned to approach the topic with that opening, but she realized it was true—depressingly true. When she saw Daniel was listening, was understanding, was genuinely interested, she went on. "I want to get married and have kids. I always have.

So I just keep waiting for it to happen. And it hasn't yet, so I feel like I haven't really started life."

"That's not true. You've got a great job, great friends—when you bother to hang out with them—you're involved in the church, you're more committed to your mom than anyone I've ever—"

"I know. I know. I don't mean my life sucks. It just feels like I'm always waiting, and I don't want to do that anymore. I want to do whatever I need to do to get what I want out of life." She wasn't going to chicken out. She was speaking the truth—the deepest truth of her heart—but she couldn't get what she wanted unless she had the courage to reach for it.

He lowered the bite he'd been about to take. "That's good. I keep telling you that you'd have better luck meeting men if you'd put yourself in the position to meet them. If you stay at home all the time, then—"

"That's not what I mean," she said, afraid the conversation would turn away from where she needed it to go. "I've tried all the dating sites and all the church singles groups, and none of them are going to work for me. I don't mean I'm chasing romance. I want a family. A stable life." Her voice broke as she added, "I want roots again, and I don't feel like I've had them forever."

Daniel's expression had sobered, and he set her plate on his empty one. "You have family, Jessica."

"I have my mom, but she..." There was no way she could continue, and she turned her head to the side to hide the sudden surge of emotion at the thought of her mom, who was declining every month, every week, every day.

When she'd controlled herself again, she turned to meet Daniel's eyes. "I don't want to be alone when she dies."

"You're not going to be alone." He was dead serious now—as serious as she was. That was one of the best things about Daniel. He didn't try to break every earnest conversation with a joke the way a lot of guys she knew did. "How can you think everyone who loves you would desert you?"

"I don't. I know my friends would be there. I know *you'd* be there. But I want more than that. I want roots. I want family. And I don't want to wait around hoping for some magical romance to happen to me so that I can get it."

He was thinking hard now. She could see it in the way his forehead had wrinkled. "So what do you want to do?"

"I have an idea," she made herself say, although the words almost choked in her throat. "One that would help both of us. One that would help both of us get our dreams."

"What are you talking about?" He narrowed his eyes and frowned. "What do *I* have to do with it?"

"Well, your dream is to be the pastor at Willow Park, right? And the only thing standing in your way is that you're not married."

"Yeah." He drew the word out slowly, his eyes searching her face. "But I'm not anywhere close to being married. I'm not even dating anyone. You know that."

He hadn't dated anyone since Lila died. He hadn't made the slightest gesture toward it. Jessica secretly suspected he'd erected an emotional shrine to Lila in his heart and nothing would ever bring it down. She glanced back over to the photo of Lila, and it seemed to affirm her conclusions.

That thought just depressed her, so she pushed it away as she continued, "I know. But I have an idea about how we can both get our dreams."

"If you've found someone to fix me up with, you know I'm not ready to…" He trailed off, as if his mind had caught up with his words and he had a glimmer of what she was about to suggest. He tensed up visibly.

"I want to move back to Willow Park too. If I have roots anywhere, it's there. And my mom's there. It's been so hard traveling every weekend to see her. I don't have time for anything but work and mom and occasionally you. I can't keep doing this indefinitely, and I don't know how long she'll…"

She didn't finish the thought since he knew the backstory as well as she did. Jessica poured every spare dollar she made into a good nursing facility for her mother in Willow Park since her mother had absolutely refused to move out of the town.

Before the marriage idea, Jessica had been considering moving back home, but financially it would be a stretch for her. Willow Park was a small town, but it drew a lot of tourists and retirees because of the mountain scenery and the historic downtown, so housing was more expensive than the suburb where she lived now. Her job allowed her to live anywhere, but paying her mother's expenses and housing in Willow Park would be a strain on her bank account.

Plus, she hadn't wanted to leave Daniel.

"So anyway," she said after clearing her throat. She wasn't looking at him now. "I was thinking there might be a solution for both of us. You need a wife. I want to put down roots and have a family."

"I'm not liking where this is going," he said in a low, gravelly voice.

She was in it now. No going back. And it wasn't as agonizingly embarrassing as she'd feared it would be. She remembered all the clear arguments she'd worked out and moved into them quickly.

"Just listen. Don't overreact until you hear the whole thing. We've been friends forever. We get along well. There's no reason to think we couldn't get along as husband and wife. You'd have a wife, or at least a fiancée, so the Session would be comfortable calling you as a pastor. And I could move back to Willow Park and have the family I want."

"You've got to be kidding, Jessica. This is absolutely insane."

"It's not insane. It solves both of our problems. Why shouldn't we consider it?"

He was almost sputtering in his outrage, which was not the reaction she'd been hoping for. Her head pounded with nerves, but she managed to keep her hands from shaking.

"Because it's not fair to you," he burst out. "I've had a real marriage, and I know I won't be blessed that way again. But you've never been married. You need to wait for the right man—someone you can really love, someone who loves you more than anything."

It hurt to hear him say that—reminded her of how in the twenty-eight years she'd been alive no man had ever been in love with her. No man had even been close.

While Lila had been alive, Jessica had been casual friends with both of them since they lived close and had come from the same hometown. She hadn't gotten close to

Daniel, however, until last year, when he'd started recovering from his grief and began spending more time with her. She'd allowed herself to hope something deeper might develop between them. It never did. He'd just never thought about her romantically at all. No man had.

She pushed the ache aside. It was an old one. Familiar.

She said, "Well, I can tell you right now that the right man for me isn't here. He doesn't appear to exist. Do you have any idea how long it's been since I've even been on a date?"

It had been an embarrassingly long time for her. Over three years since she'd even been asked out.

"That's because you don't put yourself out there. You hide away, never taking any risks, so no one is going to—"

"I don't hide away," she said, indignation overwhelming any self-consciousness. They weren't in the habit of discussing her love life, but his assumption that she could easily find a man if she just went out looking made her furious. "I work. I go to church. I do errands. I'm around for men to find me if they want. In all those dating sites and singles groups, only the losers were ever interested in me. You can't use this as an excuse. There's no sign of some mythical 'right guy' who's going to appear out of nowhere to sweep me away, and I'm not going to put my life on hold hoping and praying he'll appear. I told you I don't want to live in waiting anymore. This idea works well for me. It gets me what I want most—roots and a family. You can't use me as an excuse not to do it."

His brow had wrinkled, but she could tell he was actually thinking about it now. "I can use you as an excuse if I want."

"Well, I'm not going to listen to any of those excuses."

He was silent for a long time. Then he finally said softly, "I believe in marriage, Jessica."

"So do I. I believe in it just as much as you do. What do you think this is all about? I'm not proposing anything that would somehow undercut the nature of marriage." She took a raspy breath. "I would be faithful to you. I assume you would be too."

"Of course, I would." He looked offended at the suggestion that he would move outside the bounds of marriage—even an unconventional, practical marriage.

"So what's the problem?"

"I don't know," he admitted. He flopped back against the couch and looked rumpled and tired and bewildered. "It just seems crazy."

"That's because you haven't thought about it enough. It's really very practical, thoughtful, and reasonable. Just like me." She felt better about everything now. She'd gotten most of it said, and maybe there was a way he would agree to it.

He gave her a faint smile. "I still think I'd be getting most of the benefits, and you'd be the one cutting off your future."

"I told you already. This is the future I want."

"You'd really be okay with it?"

She could tell she was gaining ground now, and it made her blood pulse even more. "Of course. I think it's a brilliant plan. Only…"

"Only what?"

"Part of what I've always wanted is children," she admitted, looking down at her hands. "There'd be no obligation or anything, but I'd like for children to be a possibility."

She waited nervously in the silence that followed. What she'd said implied they'd have sex, and she wasn't sure how he would react to that.

"I always wanted kids too," he said at last. "Lila and I had been trying for a couple of years."

"See?" she said, pushing past the poignancy. She'd had no idea Lila and Daniel had been trying unsuccessfully to have kids. Just another heartbreaking note in their story. "It's perfect for both of us. I know you'd never admit it, but I think you want a family too. We can both get what we want."

Daniel reached over and put his hand over hers in her lap. She knew by the nature of the touch that he was trying to soften whatever he was about to say.

She was right. He said, "Jessica, you should marry a man who can love you the way you deserve."

She swallowed hard, although she'd never been deceived about his feelings for her. It didn't matter. She was serious about no longer looking for romance. Being part of a family was most important to her. "I know you don't love me romantically, but weren't you even listening? That's not the point. We love each other in the way it most matters. We're friends. We support each other. We have a good time together. We can be partners. We'd be good together as parents. I really think we would."

He let out a strange breath and glanced away from her, staring at a spot on the ground. Then he heaved himself to his feet and carried the plates into the kitchen.

She knew he was just thinking, so she didn't let his abrupt departure bother her. It wasn't a small thing she was suggesting, after all. It would change the course of both of their lives—the entire course of their futures.

When he came back, his expression had changed, and she knew he'd made his decision. She just wasn't sure what the decision would be.

He reached over and took one of her hands in both of his big, warm ones. It wasn't exactly a display of affection, more to make a serious point. He met her eyes and said hoarsely, "Jessica, promise me that you'll be happy in this sort of marriage. Promise me that being friends and partners with me in a home and family is exactly what you want out of your life. Because marriage for me is forever, no matter what the reasons for the marriage. Of course, if you want out later on, I wouldn't stop you, but I'd be committed to this for the rest of my life. This shouldn't be something either of us does lightly."

She gulped, her heart racing so wildly it hurt her ribs. For some reason, she felt closer to him in all his earnest concern and intensity than she ever had before. "I'm not doing it lightly. I'd be committed for the rest of my life too."

"So promise me that this is what you really want. I couldn't stand for you to be unhappy later on when you realize you settled, you didn't get it all."

"No one has it all. That's not the way life works. We decide what's most important to us, and we pour ourselves into that. *This* is what's most important to me. I promise this is what I want."

His lips parted slightly. A slight kink made a piece of his dark hair stick out strangely just at his temple.

No particular reason why she would have noticed that.

"I really think it *is* what you want," he breathed.

He believed her. She could see that he believed her. The tension had relaxed in his shoulders, in his eyes.

"It is," she said, trying to hold back a grin. She was so excited that she was practically hugging herself. "So what do you say? Will you marry me? You're not going to make me go down on one knee, are you?"

He couldn't quite hide an answering smile, and she knew that he'd silently said "yes."

∼

The next day was Saturday, so they went shopping for rings.

"It's too expensive," Jessica said, eyeing the diamond solitaire in the case Daniel had just asked her about. This was the third jewelry store they'd visited. Jessica kept gravitating toward the cases with the cheaper rings, but Daniel refused to consider them.

"It's an engagement ring. I'm not going to pull it out of a cereal box." Daniel was starting to look a little grumpy since their shopping expedition hadn't been very successful so far and they'd been looking now for over two hours.

"Yeah, but it's not like there's a huge romantic gesture to be made here." The store was mostly empty except for a salesman who was discreetly standing out of their way since they'd told him they would let him know when they needed help. But Jessica kept her voice low instinctively. "We shouldn't waste money on an expensive ring for me."

He slanted her an annoyed look which she dutifully ignored.

She scanned the case. All the rings looked great to her. She'd had as many romantic daydreams as any other girl about the love of her life offering a ring like these. But that wasn't what was happening here. It wasn't even what she wanted. She wanted exactly what she'd told Daniel, and she wasn't going to make up silly fantasies, even about him.

"Why don't you just buy one online?" she suggested. "You can get a better deal that way anyway."

"Would you stop that?" Daniel groaned. "I'm sorry, but I'm not going to buy an engagement ring for you without at least holding it first."

It really was very sweet—that he was taking this so seriously even though he'd never thought about her as anything but a friend. Her heart melted just a little at the sight of his stubbly, aggravated face.

"I don't even need an engagement ring," she said.

He completely ignored that comment and kept peering at the rings in the case.

"What about this one?" he asked, gesturing toward another one in the expensive display.

She tried to tug him to another case—one with more reasonably priced options. "I don't need a real diamond. What about one of these other stones? They basically look like diamonds, and they're so much cheaper."

He ignored her again. She could tell he was doing it on purpose.

Annoyed, she stepped back over and gave him a hard poke in the side. "I'm talking to you."

"You're not saying anything I'm going to take seriously. My wife is going to have an engagement ring, and it's not going to be a piece of junk."

She knew he'd been comfortable financially since he'd saved for years and didn't splurge on anything except books. But preachers never made fortunes, and he'd had to use some of his savings while he was between jobs.

"But—" She broke off when she noticed a ring in the corner of the expensive case. It was white gold with a princess cut diamond in an engraved setting. It was the most beautiful ring she'd ever seen.

She stared at it for a few seconds before she jerked her eyes away. She pointed toward another ring that was obviously much cheaper. It wasn't nearly as beautiful, but that simply didn't matter. "I like this one."

"You are the most frustrating woman on the face of the earth," he gritted out.

"You just say that because I beat you at that math competition in fifth grade even though you were two years older."

His face softened into a smile at the memory. "I'm still not sure that competition wasn't rigged."

She tried—very hard—not to laugh. Didn't exactly succeed.

"But seriously," she went on, "this ring here is perfectly nice."

"Forget it. This is futile. I'll get the ring myself, and you'll be stuck with whatever I pick out."

"Fine. Whatever you get me will be great, as long as it's not too expensive."

Daniel gave her a look as they left the store and a very confused salesman. She giggled and took his arm companionably since she knew his grumpiness was mostly for show.

The few times she'd seen Daniel genuinely angry, he'd been silent and ice cold. Just the thought of it gave her shivers.

Their normal camaraderie restored, they went to grab some coffee before they headed back to Daniel's truck.

She absolutely didn't care about the engagement ring. She was getting what she most wanted, and romance wasn't high enough on the list to matter.

∼

"Yes, I'm really getting married," she said the next day on the phone. "To Daniel. Yes, it's sudden. But you know we've always been friends, and we just realized we wanted more than that."

Her mother's voice was thin and wispy. "You're getting married?"

"Yes. In six weeks. On December 7. In Willow Park. You know I always wanted to get married in our old church."

"Who are you marrying?"

"Daniel," Jessica said patiently. Daniel was sitting across the room, working at her dining room table. They'd had dinner together so they could make plans for the wedding. He glanced over at her but then looked back at the e-mail on his laptop.

When the only response was confused silence, Jessica said, "He lived next door to us. Remember? He used to always stop by, hoping for some of your cookies or caramel corn."

"Who?"

"Daniel. He broke the window with a baseball when he was twelve."

"Oh, I know him. He's a very naughty boy. I haven't seen him lately."

"He's all grown up now. I'm marrying him."

"Who are you marrying?"

Jessica swallowed over an ache in her throat. Talking on the phone was so hard for her mother since there wasn't any face-to-face context to place the conversation. Plus it was getting late in the day. Her mom was always more disoriented in the evenings. "I'm marrying Daniel. He's going to be the pastor at First Church in Willow Park. They voted to call him as pastor today. He starts in three weeks."

"Daniel broke the window."

"Yes, he broke the window, but that was a long time ago."

After another minute, Jessica finally gave up and said good-bye.

She put her phone down and went into the kitchen, mostly just for something to do.

Bear followed her, so she leaned down to pet the dog, taking comfort in her warm, soft body and absolute loyalty.

"You okay?"

She jerked at the voice from behind her. She hadn't even heard Daniel follow her into the kitchen.

"Yeah. It's just... Mom."

"I know."

He looked understanding, sympathetic, and it meant something to her. She really would have liked a hug, but they'd never been touchy that way. There was no reason to expect it to change now.

"I just got a text from Martha. She said she'd love to do the flowers."

"Great," Jessica said, feeling better at having something to do, something to organize. "It's nice that we've known these people for so long so they're willing to work with us at the last minute. So we've got the flowers, the caterer, and the photographer. Kim is driving in on Saturday—did I tell you? She's going to help me look for a dress."

Kim had been her college roommate and had always been her best friend, aside from Daniel. She lived in Asheville now.

"Good."

She sighed. "Everyone is really excited."

"Of course they are."

"Yeah."

He took a step closer to her, nudging Bear out of the way. "We're not lying to them, Jessica. We're getting married. It's a real marriage. Our motivations are irrelevant. People are allowed to be happy for us."

"I know."

"We're not doing this at all if you're going to feel guilty about it."

"I don't feel guilty. I promise I don't feel guilty."

She didn't feel guilty. She felt a little poignant that this wasn't happening the way she'd always dreamed. But then she reminded herself of what she was getting—a home, a husband, a family, a life not always spent in waiting.

Excitement bubbled up in her heart again.

He searched her face and seemed satisfied with whatever he saw there.

Then he stuffed his hand into his pocket. "By the way, here."

She blinked as he extended his hand with a ring resting on his palm.

It was the beautifully engraved, princess-cut diamond solitaire she'd seen in the shop. The one she'd adored.

She gasped, everything in her heart reaching out for that gorgeous ring, even as she held herself very still. She managed to say, "You shouldn't have—"

"Don't even start." He sounded grumpy again, and he grabbed her left hand and pushed the ring on her finger before she could object. "There. Now we're officially engaged."

She stared down at her hands. They were pale and thin with neat, no-nonsense fingernails.

But now she had an engagement ring there.

She made sure to keep her voice dry as she said, "Yay us."

# TWO

"What do you think? The couch against the wall?"

Jessica looked from Daniel's face to the long empty wall adjacent to the fireplace in the house they'd be moving into in Willow Park. "I guess."

"You don't sound convinced."

"Wouldn't it be nicer in front of the fireplace? Like this?" She gestured toward a space in the middle of the room, walking off the length of it. "And then the TV could go here, my big chair could go here, and we could put bookcases against the wall."

She got increasingly enthusiastic about plans as she talked, but when she'd finished she looked over at him hesitantly, hoping he hadn't thought she was trying to take over. It was hard not to be excited though since it was starting to feel real—like she would really be living here in Willow Park, married to Daniel, in just a month.

"Yeah. That would be better." He grinned at her in his endearing way, causing her chest to tighten. "We are talking about *my* couch, right?"

She tried to hide a smile. "I don't know. My grandma's couch is almost an antique—" She broke off when his eyes widened in horror, and then she burst into laughter.

She'd been using her grandmother's old sofa for years because she'd never felt it worth the trouble of replacing it with something more her taste. It was perfectly comfortable but also boasted huge pink peonies all over it. Daniel's couch was only a few years old and was made of brown leather.

He narrowed his eyes as he realized she was teasing him, making her laugh even more.

The manse—the house owned by First Presbyterian Church in Willow Park and used as housing for the pastor—was charming, built about a hundred years ago, with original hardwood floors, a big front porch, and two big willows in the backyard.

Jessica had always loved the house. She couldn't believe she'd actually be living in it soon.

She couldn't believe she'd be living in it with Daniel.

They'd been engaged now for two weeks, but she still had trouble wrapping her mind around that fact.

Since they'd finished walking through the first floor, they headed upstairs to the second. Several years ago, the church had turned two small bedrooms into a master suite, and there were three other bedrooms down the hall.

Jessica was hit with the vision of having children in those rooms. All her life, she'd wanted kids, and she'd started to lose hope that she'd ever have them.

She shook off the tempting daydream. She didn't want to assume that everything would work out according to her plans.

But she couldn't help but see them. She couldn't help but hope.

"You okay?" Daniel asked, evidently noticing her distraction.

"Yeah. Good." She smiled at him, trying not to look too ridiculously happy. Most women she'd known were excited about the romance part of the marriage. She could definitely understand that. She didn't have the romance—but she'd have all the other stuff.

And that was still a lot to be excited about.

She added, "I'll make one of these bedrooms my office, if that's okay."

"Of course. Which one do you want?"

She stepped into the bedroom with two big windows, one that looked out onto the back yard. "This one, I think."

Daniel eyed the room assessingly. "I like it. You could put a desk in that corner, so you'd have a view of both windows."

"My desk wouldn't work in that corner."

"You could get a new desk. Didn't you find yours at a yard sale, anyway?"

She walked out to look through the second window. If she turned her head right, she could catch a glimpse of the charming, tree-lined street. "I'm not going to spend money on a new desk. Yard sale or not, the one I have is still fine."

He didn't argue. Just looked out the windows for a few more seconds and then wandered out of the room and down the hall to the master. She followed him since there was nothing else to see in this room.

He stopped before he walked in and cleared his throat. She suddenly realized his expression was slightly self-conscious.

"What were you thinking about the bedroom situation?" he asked.

She gulped, feeling a wave of self-consciousness washing over her, much stronger than what she'd just seen in his face. They were both adults though, and there was nothing to be embarrassed about. Not really. "Well, I guess we should probably share the master if you're okay with it. I mean, it's going to look strange to everyone if we have separate rooms."

"You'd be all right with that?"

"Why wouldn't I be?"

"I didn't know if you'd want me all in your space."

"I'll have plenty of space since you'll be working at the church most days. If we're going to be married for real, then we might as well…" She trailed off. Couldn't bring herself to say the rest.

He didn't answer, and she didn't have the nerve to look at his face. It might be hard for him—moving on after Lila, even just moving on to a half-fake marriage.

The flood of sympathy at the thought compelled her to raise her eyes. His face looked stiff, a little lost.

She put a hand on his shoulder and squeezed it. "We don't have to share a room if you'd rather not. We can work it out with how everyone else might view it."

"No. You're right. We should share the bedroom." He gave her a half smile, his mood suddenly lifting. "Besides, if we had separate bedrooms, I'm sure you'd insist on claiming the master, and I'd be stuck in one of those cubbyholes."

She giggled, relieved they'd fallen back into casual friendliness again.

No use to get nervous about sharing a bed with Daniel quite yet. Or get excited about it.

It was still a month away.

Daniel would be starting his job and moving to Willow Park next week. She wouldn't move until after the wedding.

They went into the airy master bedroom. It wasn't huge, but it was much bigger than was normally found in a house of this age, and it also had an updated attached bathroom. She couldn't help but shiver in delight at the big window and window seat against the far wall.

"My grandma's furniture would look great in here, if that's all right with you."

"Yeah. It's nicer than what I have. I can just sleep on a mattress until we get your stuff out here."

They both stared for a minute at the wall where the bed would be placed.

Jessica tried to smother the jittery excitement that arose once again at the thought of going to bed with Daniel.

To distract herself, she gestured toward one corner. "Bear's bed could go there."

The nature of the silence that followed made her shoulders stiffen. "Right?" she asked, glancing back at Daniel.

"The dog really sleeps in the bedroom?"

"Of course. And her name is Bear."

"Wouldn't she be just as happy sleeping downstairs?"

"No. She wouldn't be happy at all." All her soft, trembling feelings vanished completely in a rush of anxious indignation. "She's slept in the bedroom all her life. I'm not going to send her downstairs. She wouldn't understand. She'd probably howl and scratch at the bedroom door to get in."

Daniel sighed. "I told you that you shouldn't spoil that dog."

"What are you talking about? This is hardly an ethical issue. She's a dog, and she's perfectly well behaved. I'm not going to banish her from the bedroom. I'll sleep in another room if I have to."

Daniel's family had never had pets. His mother hadn't liked them. So he'd never grown up with a dog as a part of the family the way she had. But it didn't make sense to Jessica. He had the warmest heart when it came to people. She couldn't understand why he didn't love her sweet dog.

When he didn't reply, she added, "She's been with me for five years. I'm not going to send her away at this point. It would really hurt her feelings."

"You know dogs don't have feelings to hurt, right?"

She almost choked on her outrage. "You close the door on her face and then tell me she doesn't have feelings to hurt."

He was starting to get a little annoyed, probably thinking she was overreacting about something absolutely absurd.

But she saw him take a deep breath, obviously suppressing his initial reaction. "Fine," he said, gravel in his tone. He rubbed a hand over his thick hair. "She can sleep on her bed in here."

Jessica opened her mouth to reply but shut it again immediately.

"She does always sleep on her own bed, right?" He'd obviously picked up some sort of nuance in her silent response.

"Most of the time." She casually walked to the window and looked out on the wide expanse of backyard and the large shed. It was definitely getting to be winter, with gray skies and chilly wind. No hint of snow yet though.

Suddenly, he put his hand on her shoulder and swung her around. "Jessica?"

"I told you. She's usually sleeps on her bed."

"And the times she doesn't?"

She cleared her throat. "Sometimes she gets hot. Then she goes to the hardwood floor. It's cooler."

"Uh-huh."

They stared at each other for a long moment.

"The dog is not going to sleep on the bed with us."

"Her name is Bear."

"She's not going to sleep on the bed with us. She's huge."

"She's not that big. Don't be mean."

"*Mean*? She's almost as big as you are."

"She usually sleeps on her own bed."

"She's going to sleep on her bed all the time now. I'm going to have to put my foot down about this."

She was suddenly overwhelmed with a wave of attraction for him. Daniel was tense and annoyed and deeply authoritative. He felt really big, standing only a few inches away and glaring down at her.

She wanted him to kiss her. She wanted him to touch her.

She forced the attraction back—since he obviously didn't feel the same attraction for her. There was no use arguing about this anyway. Things would happen as they happened. "Fine. You go right ahead and put your foot down."

He blinked, obviously surprised by her response. "I'm serious about this."

"I know you are. That's why I said you could put your foot down."

He narrowed his eyes. "Something's not right here."

"Why would you say this?"

"Because you're not the most compliant of women."

Lila had been compliant. Sweet and loving and tiny and as delicately beautiful as a porcelain doll. And naturally submissive. The perfect pastor's wife. Everything Jessica was not.

But Jessica was determined to do this right—to be as perfect a pastor's wife as she could possibly be.

As long as Bear didn't get turned out of the bedroom.

"Why would you say that? I can be just as compliant as anyone else."

Daniel suddenly choked on a burst of amusement. "Arguing with me about how you're compliant is not the way to prove your point."

His amusement was infectious, but she managed not to smile—since it seemed to give him some sort of victory.

"Anyway," she concluded, "the point is that you put your foot down and that's totally fine with me. Bear sleeps on her bed. Most of the time."

∼

"You look absolutely beautiful," Martha Hendricks gushed. "I had no idea you could look so beautiful."

Martha was the wife of one of the church elders, and Jessica had known the woman all her life. Martha made sure she got her hands in any event that occurred at the church, including Jessica's wedding.

At the moment, the gray-haired woman was fluttering around a large Sunday school room, which had been turned into a dressing room for the occasion.

The wedding wouldn't start for another hour, but Jessica was already dressed. She didn't know why she was so nervous. She didn't usually get uptight about things.

But she was *really* nervous.

One of the women from church who ran a beauty salon had done Jessica's hair and makeup—curling her long straight hair until it fell in soft waves around her shoulders and applying more makeup than Jessica had ever worn in her life, although everyone assured her it looked very natural and wasn't nearly as much as most women wore for their wedding days.

She'd then put on her dress and, with nothing else to do, was left waiting the rest of the time remaining. In the past fifteen minutes, her anxiety had built up to a frantic blur.

"Thank you," she told Martha. She wasn't sure she was beautiful, but at least she looked prettier than she normally did. "What time is it?"

"One thirty," Kim said. Her friend was her only attendant since Jessica didn't have a huge circle of close friends and had almost no family. Daniel had a lot more friends, but his only attendant was his brother, Micah. "It's still a half hour until the photographer wants to do pictures."

"Okay." Restless, Jessica walked over to where her mother was sitting in a corner near the window, wearing a pale blue suit. "Are you doing okay, Mom?"

Her mother blinked at her with a familiar vague expression. "You're getting married."

It was almost a question, as if she'd just learned of the fact.

"Yeah. I'm getting married."

"To Daniel, who broke my window."

Jessica smiled, pleased her mother remembered so much and could put the pieces together today. She'd been concerned such a long outing would rattle her mother and overtire her. "Yeah. I'm marrying Daniel."

"I still can't believe it myself," Martha said, bustling around, organizing and reorganizing the bouquets that were already in perfect order since Jessica had laid them out herself. "Everyone was so surprised."

"Well, we were kind of surprised ourselves," Jessica said casually. "It just sort of happened."

"After poor Lila, we weren't sure he would *ever* move on. She was such a sweet, pretty thing—with the most angelic spirit. And you're just so different. We never would have guessed."

Jessica let out a breath and refused to let such comments bother her. She could well imagine the gossip prompted by her engagement to Daniel. She could hear the conversations about how no one could believe Daniel would choose plain old Jessica Cameron after he'd had the sweetest, most beautiful wife a man could want.

Gossip was inevitable in a small town. It was inevitable in a church—just as in any other place where people gathered. They didn't know the whole story, so they would put the pieces together as best they could.

Daniel hadn't chosen her because she was beautiful, sweet, desirable, or even good wife material.

He'd chosen her because she was convenient and he liked her.

And that was okay. This was still what she wanted. She couldn't have everything, but she could have a lot.

A knock on the door distracted her from her mental pep rally.

Kim went to answer, and she squealed when she opened the door a few inches. "Hey! Get out of here!"

Jessica instinctively stepped toward the door. "Is it Daniel?"

"No, it's Micah."

Kim said through the crack in the door, "Whatever you want can wait until after the—"

Daniel's brother was friendly and laid-back, always with an edge of laughter in his voice. "I've got something to give her. As long as she's decent, I don't know why I can't—"

"He can come in," Jessica said. "What does it matter?"

Kim and Martha reluctantly stood aside to let him enter. Micah was good-looking, about Daniel's height but with darker hair and blue eyes. He looked particularly handsome dressed in formal attire. He was just a few months older than her, but he'd always been popular in school, which she never was, so they'd never really been friends growing up. Unlike Daniel, he hadn't dropped by their house very often.

"You look great," he said, looking slightly surprised.

"Thanks." She couldn't quite keep the irony from her tone. "So do you. What did you have to give me?"

He held a small box that must be for her.

"Can we have a minute?" he asked, glancing over at Kim and Martha and then over at her mom.

It was quite clear from the other women's faces that they thought Daniel had made some sort of romantic gesture with this gift. Jessica wasn't a bit deceived on this matter, but she was still touched that he'd thought about doing something nice for her.

Jessica gestured to Kim, who helped her mother out, and Martha vacated the room too, still grumbling about how this wasn't done. It just *wasn't* done.

"So what's going on?" Jessica asked, when she and Micah were left in the room alone.

"He wanted you to have this."

She reached to take the little red box and carefully lifted the lid. Inside was a delicate gold chain from which hung a small charm. In the gold was engraved the image of a dog—one that looked a lot like Bear.

She burst into laughter, the pressure of emotion filling her chest. "Where on earth did he find this?"

"He couldn't find one he liked, so he had it custom-made."

She swallowed a sharp breath and lifted the necklace with careful fingers as if it might break. "That was so sweet of him."

"Can I tell him you think he's *sweet*?" Micah asked, a characteristic teasing note in his voice. "He'd just love to hear that."

"No. Just tell him thank you." She clasped the chain and settled the charm at her throat. Then she suddenly felt thoughtless and selfish since she didn't have a thing for Daniel.

When Micah just stood there, shifting from foot to foot, she frowned. "Was there something else?"

"Are you sure about this?" he asked.

"What do you mean?" She blinked at him, trying to push past the swell of affection for Daniel and focus on what Micah was saying.

"I mean about this." He gestured vaguely around. "Are you sure about it?"

"The wedding you mean? The marriage? Why wouldn't I be sure about it?" The affection had transformed into an odd kind of anxiety—as if she dreaded what Micah was about to say although she had no idea what it was.

"I don't know. It just seems kind of sudden."

"I've known Daniel all my life. We're not jumping into things."

Micah looked slightly uncomfortable, and he glanced away from her. She'd never seen him so serious before. "Yeah. I know. I just didn't think it was romantic between you."

"What's your point, Micah? Just get it said." She wished her voice wasn't quite so sharp, but she couldn't help it. She felt defensive, like she had to put up her guard against whatever he was about to tell her. "Do you think I'm not good enough for him or something?"

"No," he said, his eyes widening in surprise. "No, nothing like that. I was actually worried for *you*. You know Daniel. If he has something stuck in his head, he can't let it go."

She was confused now and increasingly upset, but she tried to hide it behind casual irony. "He is kind of stubborn. I know that. But what does that have to—"

"It's more than stubborn." He rubbed a hand through his hair, mussing it completely. "I mean the way he gets something in his head about the way things are supposed to be and then refuses to change his mind, no matter what. You know how he got it in his mind where he was supposed to go to college, and even when he didn't get that scholarship he expected, he still wouldn't even think about going somewhere else. He could have gone to UNC for practically nothing—they have a great program—but he wouldn't even consider it."

"I know all this. So what's your point?" She was starting to get a sense of his point though as Micah looked increasingly self-conscious. "He felt called in a certain way. The same thing with pastoring this church. He's always believed God wants him here. That's not a bad thing."

"It is when he gets an idea he won't let go of, even if it's wrong."

Jessica clenched her fists at her side, realizing now what Micah meant. Daniel had it in his mind that Lila was the wife always intended for him, and he hadn't let that go, even though she'd died. No one would ever be able to take her place in his heart. "I see…"

"Do you? I don't know if you do or not. I'm really sorry to bring all this up, Jess. It's awful timing, I know—but even though he loves you, I just don't know if he's ready to get married."

That surprised Jessica since she'd thought he'd guessed that Daniel didn't really love her. Kim was the only person she'd told about their real arrangement, and Daniel hadn't told anyone.

Micah continued, "I haven't been able to sleep, thinking about what you might be getting into. And pretty soon there won't be an easy way out." Micah looked as earnest as she'd ever seen him. "You deserve better."

She shook her head, liking this side of Micah but kind of sick about what he'd just told her.

Even though she'd already known it.

"Thank you for thinking of me," she said gently, keeping her reaction out of her voice. "I understand what you're saying, but you don't need to worry about it. Daniel and I understand each other. We have everything worked out. I know what I'm getting into, and I promise you—this is what I want."

"You're sure?" Micah's blue eyes searched her face.

"I'm sure."

"All right. You'll be good for him. I just hope he's good for you too."

A heavy knocking on the door interrupted her response. Then Daniel's voice sounded from outside. It was impossible not to recognize his warm, resonant baritone. "Micah? What are you doing in there?"

"Giving her the necklace. What do you think?"

"It's taking an absurdly long time."

"I'm done." He stepped over and kissed Jessica on the cheek. "I'll pray for you. Living with him, you're going to need it." The laughter was back in his voice, and it made her feel a lot better, like things were normal again.

Daniel said, "So get out of there. I need to talk to her too."

"No!" That was Kim from outside the door. "No peeking before the wedding."

"I need to talk to her for a minute. I'll close my eyes if I have to."

"It's fine," Jessica said, walking with Micah to the door. "He can come in. I'm not big on tradition anyway."

It wasn't true, but there was no use in getting hung up on tradition for this particular wedding. Daniel wasn't going to be blown away on first seeing her walk down the aisle.

Micah left, and Jessica was standing in the middle of the room when Daniel came in and shut the door.

He wore a black tux—no tails or bowtie since it wasn't a very formal wedding—and he looked so handsome and sophisticated she couldn't breathe for a few seconds.

She couldn't believe she was actually marrying him.

Pulling it together since no good would come from swooning over how gorgeous and masculine he looked, she asked, "So what's up?"

He didn't answer. He just stared at her with the strangest look on his face.

"Daniel?" she prompted. Maybe he was feeling guilty or uncomfortable and wanted to call the whole thing off.

She'd given up the little house she'd rented. She'd said all her good-byes in Charlotte. She'd packed up her entire life to move back here to Willow Park. Into the manse. With Daniel.

If he was about to renege on their agreement now, she might have to hit him.

"Daniel," she repeated, her voice slightly sharp. "What's the matter?"

He shook his head, as if shaking away cobwebs. "You look beautiful."

"Oh." She felt her skin warm at the compliment and what she now saw was admiration in his eyes. Her dress was fairly simple—strapless with delicate embroidery on the bodice and a full skirt without a train.

She shifted from foot to foot. "Well," she said at last. "You don't have act so flabbergasted. I can occasionally look decent, you know."

"I know." He smiled, appearing more like himself. "Aren't you cold?"

"A little," she admitted. Without thinking, she walked over to a chair, where she'd thrown the flannel shirt she'd worn that morning. She pulled it on over her dress and felt more like herself. "Is it going to snow, do you think?"

It was steel gray outside but no trace of even a stray flake yet.

"That's what they're saying." The corners of his mouth turned up slightly. "The flannel is particularly attractive."

She giggled at his dry tone and glanced down at herself. "I'll probably take it off before I walk down the aisle. Oh, and thank you for this." She put a hand over her necklace. "I love it."

He smiled again, almost tenderly. "Good."

"What did you want, anyway?"

"Is everything okay?"

"What do you mean? What did you want?"

"I just wanted to make sure you're absolutely certain about going through with this. We both take marriage seriously, and I don't want you to have acted spontaneously and then later regret it."

She liked how seriously he was thinking of her feelings, thinking of her future. "I'm not going to regret it. I know what I'm doing. I want this."

He looked at her a long time.

"Why are you so convinced I might regret it? What about you? Are you sure yourself?"

"Of course. But I've been married to a woman I loved. I've had that part of life. You never had. Are you really all right with never having it?"

For some reason, the words sliced through her chest.

She was happy about this marriage. Genuinely happy.

But she didn't need the reminder that he wasn't going to—couldn't ever—love her.

They cared about each other though, and they got along well. Most marriages throughout history had been built on far less of a foundation.

"This is what I want," she said at last. "To keep nagging me about it is to assume that I'm not capable of making an informed, reasoned decision about my own life. I *am* capable. I *am* making this decision. So you need to stop asking me about it."

He looked like he was going argue, but then his face visibly relaxed. "Right. You're right. Sorry. I'm just used to taking care of people."

"I know you are," she replied, softening despite herself. "But you don't have to take care of me. We're in this together."

"Got it."

"So we're good?"

"We're good."

"All right then. So get out of here before Martha has hysterics and stages an assault on the room."

He laughed and left, and Jessica felt better about things. They understood each other, and there was no reason they had to do things like everyone else.

It didn't matter that he didn't love her.
At least he'd thought she looked pretty.

~

When she went out to have the pre-ceremony pictures taken, Jessica suddenly realized this was real. It was happening.

Her nervousness transformed into intense anxiety, which transformed the world into a vague blur.

So she was in a blur as she posed for pictures.

And she was in a blur when they hustled her away as guests started to arrive, filling the big old sanctuary she loved.

And she was in a blur when she heard the music begin and got into position in the narthex.

And she was in a blur as she started down the aisle behind Kim, her fingers shaking as she gripped her bouquet of deep red amaryllis blossoms and even more as everyone stood in response to her entrance.

And she was in a blur as the Scripture was read, and the hymn was sung, and the homily was given by Daniel's mentor and favorite professor from seminary.

And she was in a blur as she repeated the traditional vows back to Daniel and slid the ring onto his finger.

Even when he leaned forward to kiss her, she was in a blur.

She could barely even process how it felt.

Except it was slightly scratchy from his beard.

Slightly scratchy—and not at all unpleasant.

# THREE

Forgetting about the possibility of wrinkling her wedding dress, Jessica collapsed into a chair in the Sunday school room and tried to suck down enough air to breathe.

"You okay?" Daniel asked, closing the door behind them and shutting out the rest of the wedding party.

They'd been left alone for a few minutes before the remainder of the pictures and reception.

"Yeah. It's just all so surreal." The world had finally unblurred, but now she was exhausted and strangely shaky. She was having trouble getting her mind to process what had just happened.

She'd gotten married. To Daniel. It had actually happened.

He walked over until he stood beside her, and his expression reflected concern. "Are you sure you wanted to—"

He broke off midsentence, evidently remembering he wasn't supposed to keep asking her that.

She found the energy to almost smile. "Thanks for stopping yourself. Is it hot in here, or is it just me?"

"Honestly, I feel pretty hot and overwhelmed myself."

"Really?" He looked as composed and attractive as ever, although not as slick as he had earlier. "How did you feel after your first wedding?"

When his face closed off immediately, she knew she shouldn't have asked. His marriage to Lila was still a sensitive subject—was still inviolate—and she knew better than to ask him to spill. Especially at a time like this.

She sighed and hunched her shoulders slightly, feeling more exhausted than ever.

"Not like this," he said at last.

She glanced up and saw his expression had returned to normal. At least he'd answered.

"I was completely overwhelmed that day. I think everyone is on their wedding day. But I was…"

"You were thrilled," she completed for him. She smiled at him, trying to show that she was perfectly fine with his being honest about it. She *was* perfectly fine. Trying to compete with Lila—in Daniel's heart or as a pastor's wife—would be a losing battle for Jessica, and she simply wasn't going to do it. "She was thrilled too. Everyone could see that."

"Yeah."

Ridiculously, Jessica felt almost near tears at the thought of how happy both of them had been that day eight years ago. How young they'd been. How they'd expected a lifetime together.

Why shouldn't they have expected it?

"It was a long time ago," Daniel said at last. "We both know it's not the same, but I'm happy about this too." He gestured between them to indicate their own marriage. "It's not the way it's normally done, but that doesn't mean it can't work. I think it will be good."

"Me too." Her relief must have been evident in her tone, in her smile. She stood up and put a hand on Daniel's arm, wanting to be close to him in any way she could.

He reached out and drew her into his arms.

She returned the hug immediately, instinctively, and they hugged for a long time.

She shook against him with emotion, although she wasn't sure why. Maybe it was just the aftermath of the wedding anxiety.

His arms, his body, his breath were strength to her. Warmth. Comfort. Which she needed.

There was one silly tear on her cheek when she pulled away, and she had no way to hide it.

"You okay?" he asked.

"I might scream if you keep asking me that."

He wiped the trail of the tear away with his thumb, his eyes the kindest things she'd ever seen. He didn't love her like Lila, but he *did* love her—in all the ways that were important, in all the ways she needed. She'd be a fool not to see that and appreciate it.

"I don't think I've ever seen you scream," he said, his irrepressible humor emerging at last. "It might be worth giving it a try."

Their reception was being held in the church fellowship hall. It wasn't as fancy as another venue might be, but it was a lot more convenient for their guests. The hall wasn't a gym—the kind found in a lot of contemporary churches—and it dressed up pretty nice. Since it was so close to Christmas, the florist had used clusters of poinsettias, garlands of pine and holly, and a few arrangements of red roses in the shape of Christmas trees.

Jessica was deeply relieved they'd decided against a sit-down meal since she wasn't sure she would have made it through such a long production. She wondered how women lasted through receptions that stretched late into the evening after the stress of a wedding.

She rushed the photographer through the pictures since she'd been to far too many weddings where she'd had to wait bored at the reception for ages before the bride and groom finally made an appearance and she could go home. Then she put on her favorite part of her wedding ensemble—an adorable fake-fur shrug—and she and Daniel went to the fellowship hall to greet their guests.

She still felt the same jittery excitement she'd been feeling since they'd gotten engaged, intensified now that the wedding had actually happened, but she was also overwhelmed with the idea of so many people waiting to hug and congratulate her. She didn't like being the center of attention, and constantly smiling was starting to hurt her face.

To give herself motivation, she kept telling herself that she and Daniel just needed to make the round of greetings. Then they could cut the cake.

Then she could get out of here.

"You look so beautiful," Miss Ross, her second-grade teacher, said, giving her a hug.

"Thank you." Each conversation was almost exactly the same. She wasn't sure she looked beautiful anymore since the waves in her hair had flattened and her makeup had mostly worn off, but people kept telling her so anyway.

"We weren't sure you were *ever* going to get married."

She'd heard the same sentiment so many times—this week, this month, and the past several years of her life—that she didn't let it bother her anymore.

Willow Park was a small town in an area with traditional values. It didn't matter that she had a good career and her independence. She would be incomplete in their eyes until she got married. As wrong as she believed that to be, she tried not to hold it against them.

Daniel put a hand on her back in a possessive gesture she really liked. So what if they weren't blissfully in love? They were partners in this. They understood each other. And they could be happy.

"She was just waiting for the right man," he said, amusement in his voice.

Jessica smiled up at him, probably looking rather fatuous. "That's right. Who would have guessed it was the boy next door?"

"Isn't there a song about that?" Miss Ross asked.

Jessica knew her musicals, and without thinking, she sang a few bars from the song Miss Ross was referring to from *Meet Me in St. Louis*.

She was no Judy Garland, but she was at least on key.

Then she realized everyone around her had stopped to listen, and Daniel was smiling in appreciative surprise.

She broke off. "Sorry. Is that the song you meant?"

There was a smattering of applause and laughter, and Daniel slid his arm around her waist and pulled her to his side.

"You should sing more often," he said.

She felt vaguely pleased by the reaction, but she wondered why she'd burst into song that way.

All her life, she'd made sure she stayed out of the spotlight. That wasn't going to change now.

∼

That evening, she took a long shower, shaving carefully and spending more time in the bathroom than she ever had in her life.

She and Daniel were spending the night in the house.

They'd gotten all her stuff moved in last week, and he'd been living here for the past three weeks. They'd agreed there was no reason to go to a hotel for their first night as man and wife.

They weren't doing a honeymoon. Daniel had just started his job, and he couldn't take time off during the Christmas season anyway—one of the high points of the church calendar. Plus Jessica couldn't help but think a honeymoon would be a waste of money.

Maybe later they could take a vacation together once they were comfortable with being married to each other. But right now it would be awkward. It would place pressure on their marriage they didn't need.

So their first night would be in their own bed in their new house.

She brushed her hair, which she'd kept out of the water in the shower, and put on her new nightgown.

She wasn't about to wear anything overtly sexy or romantic since she didn't want Daniel to think she was trying to turn the evening into something it wasn't. So the gown she'd bought for tonight was simple and blue with lace straps and a ribbon that tied off under her breasts.

It wasn't likely to take Daniel's breath away, but it was pretty, and it matched her eyes.

She tried not to stare at him as she emerged from the bathroom. He'd taken a shower before her, and now he was half under the covers, propped up on pillows, bare-chested, and reading a book.

She wasn't looking in his direction, but she felt his eyes on her as she went to the corner where Bear was begging at the base of the dresser.

Jessica picked up the bone which she'd placed on top of the dresser earlier and motioned to Bear's bed.

The dog eagerly scrambled to the bed and greeted the bone with enthusiastic mouth noises.

"Now, you stay," Jessica told Bear as she turned back toward her own bed. Bear was usually well-behaved and probably wouldn't try to leap onto the bed to join them tonight.

Hopefully not, anyway.

Daniel was still watching her as she approached. "Are you tired?" he asked. She couldn't read the expression in his eyes.

She shrugged. "A little. Not too bad." She'd been exhausted earlier during the reception, but now she felt too wired and jittery to be tired. "What about you?"

"I'm fine."

"What are you reading?"

"Bonhoeffer."

She gave a breathy laugh. "A little light reading before bed?"

"He's pretty compelling."

"I'm sure. You can keep reading if you want. The light won't bother me."

She felt rather adrift all of a sudden though. She'd assumed they'd have sex tonight, but maybe Daniel would rather read.

She wasn't anyone's dream wife, after all. She thought she was attractive enough, but she doubted any man had ever had sexual fantasies about her. They usually didn't think about her at all.

When he just looked at her some more, she gulped. "Seriously. You can read, if you'd rather…"

"If I'd rather read than what?"

Her cheeks warmed, but she was determined to be adult and mature about this topic. "Well, I was thinking we might… we might have sex. But we really don't have to."

"I didn't know if you'd want to right away." He placed the book on the nightstand, which was an immense relief. At least he didn't prefer Bonhoeffer to having sex with her. "We can take some time to get used to things before we have sex if you'd be more comfortable with that."

She gave him a faint smile. "We've known each other all our lives. I know you. I trust you. Sex is one of the… one of the perks of marriage, so I figure there's no reason to wait. Unless you don't want to."

"Why wouldn't I want to?"

"I don't know."

"I could ask you the same thing. We've always just been friends, and I'm not any sort of dream man. I didn't even know if you'd be attracted to me."

She realized he was serious—that he had no idea how incredibly handsome and irresistible and sexy he was. And not just to her. Women *always* noticed Daniel.

"You look pretty good to me," she said without thinking. He looked more than good without a shirt on, his shoulders broad, his abs tight, and a scattering of dark hair on his chest that she felt the sudden desire to touch.

His mouth tightened with suppressed amusement, and she blushed even deeper. But she pressed on, "But you've never been attracted to *me*, so if you're not... if you're not into it, that's totally fine. It won't hurt my feelings."

It might hurt her feelings *a little*, but she absolutely wasn't going to take it personally. If this was going to work, then they couldn't put pressure on each other.

"I can be into it. That's not a problem."

"Oh. I just didn't want to assume that cliché about men always wanting sex, no matter who or what—"

"Don't assume that cliché. It's not true. But I can definitely be into this."

She raised her eyes in surprise and saw he looked almost sheepish.

"You look pretty good to me too," he said, something thicker in his tone that made her breath hitch.

They smiled at each other—completely understanding each other—and Jessica's excitement returned with full force.

"Okay," she said, feeling pleased and gratified that he was attracted to her like she was to him. "So we got all this worked out then?"

"Yeah. I think so."

"So sex tonight?"

He nodded, a warm look in his eyes that made her shiver. "Sex tonight." Then his expression changed. "Are you a virgin?"

She blinked. "Yeah. You know I believe in waiting until marriage."

She knew he believed the same thing. She was pretty sure Lila was the only woman he'd slept with before tonight.

"I know. But people can believe it and still not be able to hold themselves to it. I would understand. You know that, right? I mean, I would never judge—"

"I know. I know that. I know you'd never judge. But it's true." She ducked her head. "I waited."

His face had softened when she darted her eyes up to him again. "Okay. I don't want you to be nervous. I'll try to be gentle."

She crawled under the covers as he reached over to turn off the light on his nightstand. The room wasn't pitch black, and she could see him move beside her.

To cut the sudden tension she felt, she said, "There's no reason to be *too* gentle. I don't think I'm going to break."

He laughed—his deep, familiar laugh. She suddenly realized she should try harder to be sexy and romantic rather than making him laugh.

She tried to think of something sexier to say, but everything that came to her mind seemed absolutely ridiculous. Cheap, shallow words. Not like her—or him—at all.

There was no sense in putting on a show anyway. This wasn't the consummation of a great romance, and it wasn't likely to be the kind of sex that blew the roof off the house.

It was just them.

She'd barely resolved herself to this reality when he moved over her and edged down to kiss her softly.

She'd kissed men before, but only a few and not very often, so she wasn't very experienced. Even his lips moving gently against hers now felt new, strange, exciting. He smelled like soap, and she tried to relax into the kiss.

His tongue delicately glided over the line between her lips. When she parted them for him, he licked lightly across the undersides.

It felt increasingly good. Made her breath quicken and her blood pound. She reached up to tangle her fingers into his thick hair.

She was just getting into it—starting to get the hang of it—when he moved away, but only to trail little kisses over her face and down her neck.

She gave a sharp gasp when he found a sensitive spot at the base of her throat.

"How is it, Jessica?" he murmured against her skin.

"Good." She gave another gasp as his tongue fluttered against that same spot. "I like it."

"Can I take your gown off?"

"Of course." It made her a little nervous again, but it was dark in the room. Her body was okay—long and slim—but it wasn't anything special.

She helped him pull the gown over her head and then shuddered when his mouth moved down to her naked breast.

"Oh!" she gasped, grabbing at his head instinctively.

He flicked her nipple with his tongue, sending little tugs of pleasure shooting down between her legs.

As his mouth moved against her flesh, another sensation joined the first one. She shuddered in the wake of it. Then arched up as he nuzzled between her breasts.

She tried to hold it back, but a little giggle escaped her lips.

He raised his head. "What are you laughing at? I might be out of practice, but surely I'm not *that* bad at it."

She bit her lip, silently cursing her lack of control. She really hoped he wasn't offended. "You're not bad at it at all. Your beard tickles."

It was the truth, so she might as well admit it. Maybe it wouldn't spoil the mood too much.

He chuckled, obviously not offended. "If it really bothers you, I can shave it. But I don't think it will tickle for long."

She blushed red hot when she realized the implications, and pressure tightened at her groin. Not wanting him to get the best of her though, she said, "That sounds kind of smug. I'm not sure I've seen any cause yet for you to be—"

She broke off with a ragged gasp when he grazed her nipple with his teeth.

"What were you saying?" he asked, a delicious kind of texture to his tone.

"Don't be smug." She wanted to laugh, which was so strange since she was quickly growing aroused at the same time.

He kissed and fondled her for several minutes, and it wasn't long until his beard tickling was the last thing on her mind.

She'd never felt like this in her life—like she couldn't quite control the motion of her body. Her hips kept rocking restlessly, and she was stroking and clutching at Daniel's back, head, and chest. She started making silly little sounds, although she tried to stifle them since they made her self-conscious.

Something visceral was changing in Daniel's body too. She couldn't quite pinpoint the signs of the change since he was still caressing her very carefully and often checking to make sure she liked it.

But he was tenser now as he moved on top of her, and his touch wasn't quite as controlled. He took her breast in his mouth again, but this time it felt more eager, more excited.

She pressed up into his mouth, pushing his head down to hold it in place as he suckled. It felt so good—and so frustrating at the same time—that she couldn't hold back a soft sobbing sound. One of her legs had somehow wrapped around his hips, although she wasn't conscious of moving it, and she found herself shamelessly rubbing herself against his hip to ease the ache at her center.

As she rubbed, she found something else, so she rubbed against that too.

He groaned against her breast, his body tightening palpably at her motion.

"Do you think you're ready, Jessica?" he asked, jerking his head up and straightening his arms.

"Yeah," she gasped. "Oh yeah. Please."

She sounded too eager, but there was absolutely no way to hide her response.

She wanted him so badly she might scream. She'd never realized she was capable of feeling this way.

He groaned again, with a different resonance this time, and he repositioned himself above her so he was lying between her legs and his head was just over hers.

"Are you sur—"

"Yes," she said, practically clawing at his back to get him in position. "Hurry up. I'm dying here."

He gave a huff that sounded like laughter.

Then she suddenly wondered if he would prefer a woman who was more innocent and passive, who would let him take control. Maybe that was how Lila had been—since she'd been sweet and compliant in all other areas of her life.

She didn't dwell on the question or comparison though. Even if that was what Daniel would prefer, Jessica just couldn't be that way.

When he kissed her mouth again, she responded passionately, tugging at his hair and tangling her tongue with his.

He wasn't as careful as he'd been when he'd kissed her earlier. He devoured her mouth, making husky sounds in his throat as the embrace deepened.

She rocked up into him as they kissed, mimicking the motion of lovemaking. Increasingly desperate for relief, she reached down to grab the waistband of his pajama pants and tried to push them down over his lean hips.

He pulled out of the kiss enough to help her, but after he'd rid himself of the pants, he was kissing her again.

Her mind was a blur of sensation and excitement, and she couldn't seem to catch her breath.

Then she suddenly felt his hand between her thighs, exploring until he'd slipped a finger inside her.

She gave a breathless little cry and arched up at the sensation.

"You're ready."

She didn't know if it was a question or a statement. Either way, it should be pretty obvious she was ready. "Yeah. Oh yeah."

"Do we need any—"

She knew what he was asking, so he didn't need to finish. "I started birth control after we got engaged." She might want kids, but not yet—not before they got used to being married to each other.

He repositioned himself again, putting more weight on his knees. Then he took his erection in his hand and lined himself up at her entrance.

"It might not be that great for you this time," he said, his voice almost rough with texture. Even in the dim room, she could see his dark eyes searching her face, looking for any signs of discomfort or hesitation, despite how obviously excited he was.

"I know. I know how things work. I'm ready."

Then he started to enter her.

He didn't go in all at once, the way she'd been expecting. He slid in and out, just at her entrance, in a series of fast little thrusts. He kept up the same kind of motion, in and out, slightly reangling, as he went increasingly deep.

It felt really good until he was almost all the way in. Then the pressure became genuinely uncomfortable.

"You okay?" he asked, when she arched up automatically.

"Remember what I said would happen if you kept asking me that?"

"Are you going to scream?"

"Maybe."

"Are you really okay?"

"Yeah. I'm okay."

He was holding himself still now, supported by straightened arms. "Does it hurt?"

"Not really. Just pressure. It's going to be fine."

The discomfort had taken the edge off her arousal though, so she was a little disappointed as she breathed slowly to relax her body.

She supposed it was too much to expect to be swept away by passion on her very first time. She wasn't a silly girl with unrealistic fantasies about this. Things didn't have to be perfect to still be good.

He pulled out, relieving the pressure. Before she could object to his retreat, he entered her again, using the same in-and-out penetration. It was better this time—didn't hurt nearly as much.

"Okay?" he asked. His arms were shaking slightly as they supported his weight above her, and she could feel heat radiating off him.

"Yeah. It's good." Not wanting him to get distracted by worrying about her, she pulled his head down into a kiss.

He kissed her back immediately, his tongue thrusting rhythmically into her mouth.

She responded with her own tongue and then with her body. Her hips rocked up into his, shifting his erection inside her in a way that felt so deep, so strange.

He groaned thickly as he broke the kiss. Then he started to move over her, pumping his hips until, with a few starts and stops, they'd established a rhythm.

He was really into it now. He started to make grunting noises, and his body shook with tension beneath her hands. She held on to him and tried to match his thrusts, although she wasn't sure she was doing a really good job.

She wanted him to enjoy it. It wasn't as uncomfortable now, and other sensations were starting to build. Although not very fast and not with the intensity they'd had before he'd entered her.

"Jessica," he rasped, his motion accelerating even more. "Jessica."

She made a little whimper of pleasure, both from their motion and from the way he was saying her name.

She bent her legs, bringing her knees higher as he changed positions slightly.

"How is it?" he managed to huff, although in the dim light his face twisted in effort.

He was sweating. She could feel the dampness under her palms as she stroked his back.

She was touched that he was so concerned about her enjoying it too, even as he was pretty far gone. "It's good. It's so good." She cried out as she felt a sharp jolt of pleasure, completely unexpectedly. "So good. So good."

He leaned down to kiss her again, but he obviously didn't have much coordination left. Neither did she. Their mouths moved clumsily together for a minute before he raised himself on his arms again.

His motion was almost wild now. "I'm not sure I can hold out—"

"It's fine." She felt so odd, so overwhelmed, like she might cry. "I'm good. I want you to come."

He released a long moan as his hips jerked against hers. Then he moaned again, differently, as his body suddenly froze and then released.

She loved how it felt—loved how he'd taken such pleasure in her, loved that she could give it to him.

She felt closer to him than she ever had before when his body slowly relaxed and he lowered himself over her.

She hugged him against her, and he mumbled out words she couldn't quite understand as he pressed kisses into her neck and jaw.

She responded when he kissed her mouth, softly now, without the urgency of before. Then she was surprised when he reached down to stroke her hip and thigh. When he pulled out of the kiss, his other hand slipped up to her left breast.

"What are you doing?" she asked, shifting a little under his touch. "I thought it was over."

"It was over for me, but I think I enjoyed it more than you did."

She sucked in a sharp breath when his head moved down to her breast. "You don't have to do—"

One hand slid between her thighs to explore. She was wet from her earlier arousal and his release, and her flesh was still sensitized and pulsing. "It's not about having to," he said in a low voice. "It's about *wanting* to."

Her body was reacting, was already trying to work into an instinctive rhythm. She stretched her back and inhaled sharply as his fingers fondled her intimately.

She felt a swell of deep affection at how serious he was about pleasing her. She grabbed at his shoulders and held on. He evidently knew exactly what he was doing. Two fingers were pumping in and out of her tight channel, while his thumb massaged her with deep precision. He matched that pattern with his mouth on her breast, and so she felt dual tugs, dual sensations building inside.

"Daniel," she groaned, her voice barely recognizable. "Daniel, it's so good. Do it just like that."

Her hips were starting to thrust into his motion, deepening the sensations, accelerating the rhythm, but she wanted to feel close to him in a different way.

"Daniel," she gasped, pumping her hips faster, pulling him up. "Daniel, want to… kiss you."

She whimpered when he adjusted up and captured her lips with his mouth.

Then it was his kiss, his touch, his rhythm—all working together in unison. He began to curl his fingers inside her, and her whole body shuddered in response. She felt the sensations coalescing, building, mounting, swelling toward that one moment of release. She was damp with perspiration and panting under his mouth. Right at the moment before she climaxed, he pulled his head up out of the kiss.

She knew he was watching as her hips jerked erratically, as her face contorted in pleasure, as her upper body came flying up in a momentum she couldn't control. She cried out hoarsely and clawed at the skin on his bare shoulders. Her muscles clamped down violently around his fingers, but he sustained his steady motion until the contractions stopped completely.

"Oh, oh, oh, fuck," she groaned as her body relaxed in delicious release.

Her eyes were closed, but it felt like he was smiling.

Then her eyes flew open and she clamped a hand over her mouth. "Oh, I didn't mean to say that!"

He burst into uninhibited laughter.

"I *never* say that," she said, her face reddening even more than it had been.

He was still laughing as he pulled her against his chest in a half hug. "I know you don't. But this is one of the few times when the word is actually appropriate."

"Well, you don't have to laugh at me. It just slipped out. It wasn't *that* funny."

"Yes, it was."

She couldn't help but smile at his laughter and at the feel of his warm body against hers.

"Thank you," she said at last. "For doing that for me, I mean."

"You're welcome. I enjoyed it. All of it."

"Good. Me too."

She felt incredibly pleased with herself, with him, with the whole situation.

"How do you feel?" he asked, shifting slightly.

"Good. A little sore, but good. What about you?"

"Good."

For some reason, the smile had left his voice. She didn't know why, but she felt something shift in the mood between them.

She wasn't sure what either of them would have said, but the silence was interrupted by a familiar scratching sound.

Bear, trying to make a nest on her bed by scratching the living daylights out of it.

"Bear," she said. "Enough."

Bear ignored her, as usual. The dog was fairly obedient, but scratching up a nest was serious business and always the priority.

"What is she doing over there?" Daniel asked, sitting up in bed and peering over in the dark room toward the dog.

"She's trying to get her spot right. Don't sound so impatient with her."

"It sounds like she's digging her way through the floor."

"She's not going to hurt the floor." Worried Daniel would get annoyed, Jessica hauled herself out of bed and limped over to the dog. She patted Bear's back until the dog settled down.

Since she was up, she went to the bathroom and cleaned herself up a little.

She was still limping slightly as she returned to bed.

"You okay?" Daniel asked as she climbed in beside him.

She didn't answer. Just gave him a speaking look that she was sure he could read even in the dark.

"You're limping."

"I'm a little sore. It's not that bad."

Maybe she should act more delicate and get him to take care of her, but she'd never been any good at doing that.

She scooted toward him and was relieved when he wrapped an arm around her.

It felt nice, to sleep against him. Almost as nice as their lovemaking had been.

She'd thought for a long time that she'd never have a man to sleep against.

~

It had been a really long day, and she fell asleep almost immediately.

She woke up around two in the morning, however, and rolled instinctively toward Daniel's side of the bed.

It was empty.

It took a moment to orient herself, but this was indeed the master bedroom of the manse, and Bear was snoring softly from her corner.

Daniel just wasn't in bed.

The bathroom door was opened, so he wasn't in there. Concerned, she got out of bed and walked barefoot out to the hall.

The other bedrooms were all empty, so she went downstairs.

She found him in the small room they'd made his study, where he'd set up walls of bookcases and placed his old desk.

He sat at his desk, reading his Bible. She couldn't tell if he was doing devotions or trying to work.

"What are you doing?" she asked.

He jerked, obviously surprised by her presence. "Nothing. Just reading. You should go back to bed."

"Why are you reading down here in the middle of the night?"

"I couldn't sleep."

She frowned, wondering if he'd always been in this bad habit of getting up in the wee hours or if tonight was somehow special. He'd never had workaholic tendencies—at least none she'd been aware of. "You need to rest. This can't be good for you."

He smiled, but his expression was a little distant. Not like earlier at all. "I'm fine, Jessica. Seriously. Go on back to bed."

She understood his resonance clearly. She wasn't welcomed in his study—not at the moment anyway. She started to turn away.

She was very inexperienced with sex. Very inexperienced with marriage. Very inexperienced with *men*.

But she was sure—she was absolutely sure—this wasn't right.

She turned back. "Can't you do that later? You should come to bed."

He released a long sigh and straightened up. She could see from his expression that he was trying to think of an excuse, a reason not to return to bed with her.

As he thought, his eyes rested on a framed picture on his desk. The photo of Lila. He must have pulled it out tonight since he hadn't set it up in his study before.

When he saw she'd noticed the photo, he silently slid a drawer opened and started to put the picture away.

"You don't have to put it up," she said in a rush, her heart aching for so many reasons. "I'd never want you to hide her picture. I'd never want you to pretend she wasn't important to you."

His features twisted—strangely, in a way she almost never saw. He was nearly always in control, of his words, his behavior, even his facial expressions. "It doesn't seem right— to keep her photo out like this when I'm married to you. I don't want you to ever think I don't... I don't want to hurt you."

She *was* hurt, but it was irrational. Their lovemaking had felt intimate, important to her. It had made her want to be even closer to him. But it must have been different for him since he'd run away from her. She'd like to think she was first in his heart, but she was never going to have that role. It was okay. She'd known what she was getting into, and she wasn't going to create tension between them when none had to exist.

"I know you'd never try to hurt me." In her earnestness, she walked into the study and toward his desk. She reached over to retrieve the framed picture and set it up on the desk. "I know you care about me, Daniel, but I care about you too. And I know you still miss her. I know she's still important to you. You can keep her picture out. We both know this isn't a regular marriage."

"It *is* a marriage." He gazed up at her, and for just a moment she thought she saw something like yearning in his eyes. Then it disappeared, so she decided she must have been wrong.

There was no reason for Daniel to yearn for her. If he wanted her, he could have her. He only had to reach out.

"I know it's a marriage, but it's only going to work if we're honest with each other. So keep her picture out for as long as you need to. Seriously."

He swallowed hard and nodded, his eyes returning to his opened Bible. She could see now that he'd been reading in Psalms.

"So if we're being honest with each other," she added, "I really want you to come back to bed. Please?" she added, a slight plea in her tone.

He let out another breath—this one different than before—and his face softened in a way she recognized, that reflected how much he liked her, how much he wanted her to be happy. "Okay."

He got up from his desk, turned out the lights in the study, and went back to bed with her. He even held her for a few minutes before he rolled away to go to sleep.

Jessica felt better as she closed her eyes again. Their marriage wasn't normal. It wasn't perfect. But maybe they could still make this work.

# FOUR

It was just after six when Jessica woke up and headed to the kitchen to look for coffee with Bear at her heels.

Daniel was leaning against a counter, chugging down water. He'd obviously just gotten back from his regular morning run because he was dripping with sweat.

"You're up early," he said, lowering the bottle and moving out of the way so she could reach the coffee pot.

"Not as early as you." She'd known he usually woke up early to run, but she didn't know it was *that* early.

"Did you sleep all right?" she asked. She'd woken up once at around four, and he'd been sound asleep then, so she hoped he slept well for the hours he was actually in bed.

"Yeah." He wiped his damp face with the bottom of his T-shirt. Then he gave Bear a quick pat on the head since the dog had come over to greet him eagerly. It seemed more like a gesture than a genuine greeting on his part, but it was better than nothing. "Do you feel okay?"

She drew her brows together in confusion until she realized he was asking about how she felt after sex the night before. She felt a shudder of self-conscious pleasure at the memory of how she'd let go and at how Daniel had let go too. "Yeah. I feel pretty good."

"Good." He gave her a little smile. "I've got to shower."

Something about him seemed a little strange this morning. He was as kind as always, but also a little distant.

Not like the Daniel she was used to. "Okay. I'm going to take Bear for a walk."

When she got back to the house forty-five minutes later, Daniel was dressed for Sunday, doing his devotions, and eating a protein bar with his coffee in the study, so she didn't disturb him.

She turned on the oven and wished she could bake. Lila had always been a wonderful cook. She'd also sewn her own pillows and curtains, and she'd been an amazing hostess, even for casual get-togethers. Her home was always beautifully cleaned and welcoming—she was the perfect pastor's wife.

Jessica knew she couldn't equal Lila's domestic prowess. She was anything but amazing in the kitchen, and her cleaning was mostly perfunctory. But she was excited about the new challenge and didn't want Daniel to regret his decision to marry her, so she was committed to doing everything she could to be the kind of pastor's wife she'd always seen.

As a first step, she pulled out pop-out cinnamon rolls from the refrigerator. Then she lined them on the baking sheet and stuck them in the heated oven.

As they cooked, she fixed herself a bowl of cereal and ate it at the kitchen table with Bear for company.

She was icing the rolls when Daniel returned to the kitchen, his suit jacket draped over his arm. "Something smells good."

"I made cinnamon rolls for Sunday morning."

"Yum." He reached over her shoulder and snatched one she'd just iced.

"Wait! It's hot."

He ate it in three bites. "Not too hot. Thank you."

"You're welcome." She smiled since he seemed to genuinely appreciate her effort.

He washed his hands, which were sticky from the icing, and then pulled on his jacket. "I've got to get to church."

"Already? It's barely seven thirty." Sunday school didn't start until nine thirty, and the church was just over a mile away.

"Yeah. I've got some prep still to do. I'll see you at Sunday school."

"Okay," she said as he left the house. She wasn't going to be annoyed or frustrated. Sunday morning was the climax of the work week for pastors, and maybe Daniel needed some privacy to get himself prepared and together.

He'd hadn't been at the church for very long, after all, and he would want to do a good job.

This whole thing wasn't about her. He'd been perfectly nice to her this morning. She wouldn't be upset because he'd felt a little distant.

She sighed as she looked down at the four remaining cinnamon buns. Then she glanced at Bear, who was begging patiently just beside them. "Do you want a cinnamon roll?" she asked the dog. "There's no way I can eat all these."

Bear didn't have an answer for her, but she wasn't about to leave the food.

~

Daniel had been installed as pastor of the church for a few weeks now, but this was the first Sunday Jessica had attended since he'd arrived.

Everyone greeted her warmly, repeating that she and Daniel really should have taken the Sunday off.

Despite all the comments, Jessica figured it was just as well to jump right into figuring out their life together.

She'd heard Daniel preach—many, many times—since she'd often attended the small church outside Charlotte he'd been pastor of before. No one was like Daniel in the pulpit. He made the Bible come alive—with intelligence and deep knowledge and passion and gravity and authority. Somehow, all those things at once.

He might be tired this morning, but there was no evidence of fatigue in his manner or voice. She felt an odd sense of possessive pride as she watched him.

He was her husband. Her *husband*. This amazing man.

They went to the house of one of the elders for lunch after the service. Jessica would not have chosen to spend the afternoon socializing, but Daniel said they needed to go since the elder—Chip White—still wasn't fully convinced Daniel had the wisdom and experience to pastor the church.

It was part of being married to a pastor. You had to have Sunday lunch with families from the congregation when they invited you—whether you felt like it or not.

So she didn't complain at all on the half-hour drive to the farmhouse where the White family lived. And she didn't make any of the hints about leaving she was tempted to make, even when the visit lasted well past three o'clock and she was aching with fatigue.

They made it home just after four, and Jessica was ready to slump to the floor.

"Thanks for going with me," Daniel said, obviously recognizing she was tired. They were in the bedroom to change out of their Sunday clothes.

"Of course I'd go. What did you expect?"

"Well, I appreciate it anyway. It's been a really long weekend. You look like you need some rest." He took off his jacket and tie and started unbuttoning his shirt.

She felt a jittery excitement as he undressed in front of her, evidently not even self-conscious about it. It felt intimate in a way she just wasn't used to. "You do too. You must be even more exhausted than I am."

She sat on the bed and slid off her shoes.

"I'm not that tired."

"You had to preach this morning, and you didn't get much sleep last night."

"You're not going to start nagging now that we're married, are you?" He pulled his white T-shirt over his head, baring a very attractive abdomen, and undid his pants.

"I'm not nagging." She tried very hard to focus on the topic at hand and not on the sudden desire to pull Daniel into the bed with her. "But it's Sunday. There's no reason why you shouldn't rest."

"I don't take naps."

"Well, then at least—"

"Jessica, enough." The words weren't harsh or angry, but they were much terser than she normally heard from him.

She jerked back in response to his tone.

Obviously seeing her reaction, his expression changed immediately. "I'm sorry. I didn't mean to snap at you. I'm really sorry."

"It's fine. Don't worry about it." She was more upset than she should have been, mostly because she didn't know what had prompted his sudden shift in mood. He'd felt a little distant today, but nothing that would explain such an unusual response. "I guess maybe I was nagging a little."

"You weren't really." He sat down on the bed beside her and put his hand on her knee.

She relaxed, feeling like she knew him again. "So what are you going to do this afternoon?"

"I've got some reading to do."

"Oh." That didn't sound bad. Reading was restful, after all. "Okay."

"And I've got a project to do out in the workshop."

He'd turned the shed in the yard into a kind of workshop where he'd put all his tools. As with cars, he liked to fiddle around with carpentry. Jessica wasn't sure how good he really was at it since his projects didn't always turn out the way he planned. Micah, who was a contractor, never got tired of mocking his brother's efforts. But Daniel enjoyed his attempts anyway.

"What are you working on?"

"This and that," he said noncommittally as he pulled on a pair of worn jeans. "Thanks again for coming to lunch with me."

"You don't have to thank me for that." She tried not to sound frustrated, but surely he hadn't expected her to be his wife and then not perform any of the duties that came with it.

He half smiled. "Okay."

When he left the room, she picked up the suit he'd tossed on the bed. It was still in good shape and didn't need to be dry-cleaned yet, so she hung it up. His shirt was not in good shape, so she put it in the laundry. Then she changed into something more comfortable than her skirt and sweater set.

When she went downstairs, she saw Daniel's study door was closed.

Evidently, he was going to read in there.

∼

The next day, Jessica stopped working in time to fix a lunch for her and Daniel.

He'd said he would just grab something for lunch, and she knew enough about his habits to understand this meant he would eat a protein bar or a bag of nuts for lunch.

So she made a sandwich—one she knew he would like with turkey, ham, bacon, lettuce, mayonnaise, and dijon mustard on it—and a salad and then packed it all up with some cookies in a Baggie to take over to the church.

Despite his study at home, he also needed to keep an office at church to work and meet with members of the congregation. He'd set up his with a good computer, a wall of bookshelves with all his biblical commentaries and sermon preparation books, and a conference table.

He was working at the computer with a big commentary and his Bible open on his desk when she tapped on his half-opened door.

He turned in his desk chair and looked surprised when he saw her. "Hey. What are you doing here?"

"I brought you lunch."

"Why?"

She frowned. If every nice thing she did for him was going to be treated to an inquisition, it was going to get old fast. "Because you didn't have a lunch."

Daniel gestured toward a bottle of water and a protein bar, untouched on the surface of his desk.

"That's what I thought," she said, coming over to unpack the bag she'd brought.

She pulled up a chair and sat down near the desk so he wouldn't go back to working and forget about eating.

He smiled as he unwrapped the sandwich. "Did you make this for me?"

"Yes."

"Don't you need to be working?"

"I'm allowed to stop for lunch."

"I guess so. But you really didn't have to go to the trouble. You work too, so you don't have to always get meals for us. I'd never expect you to—"

"What trouble? It took exactly five minutes and then two minutes to drive over here."

"I guess so. Thank you."

"You're welcome."

He slanted her a look. "Are you annoyed with me?"

"No."

"You look like you might be annoyed."

"I'm not annoyed. As long as you actually eat your lunch."

He closed his Bible and commentary and moved them out of the way. Then he gave silent thanks for the meal and started to eat.

Jessica relaxed and pulled out her own sandwich.

His mouth twitched slightly when he glanced at her. "You better be careful. I might start to expect you to bring me lunch every day."

"Some days you'll have to come home for lunch, and then it will be hit-or-miss about what you get."

"I have lunch meetings a lot anyway. A lot of men in the congregation can only meet to talk at lunchtime."

"So that's fine. Occasionally, I might bring you lunch."

He smiled at her as he swallowed a bite, and she smiled back—feeling like he was her friend again and not this slightly unknowable husband he'd become.

"What are you working on?" she asked, gesturing toward the computer.

"Next week's sermon."

"How's it going?"

"I've not done as much as I hoped. People keep stopping by to talk."

"Oh. Sorry."

"I didn't mean you."

"Okay. Good. Are people just congratulating you on the wedding?"

"Mostly. Chip stopped by though."

"Was he complaining again?"

"Not as directly. He just wants to cut back on the programs for Christmas."

"Why? People will be disappointed if we don't do everything we usually do."

"I know. He thinks it's too much logistically with the transition. He means he doesn't think I'm up for the job."

"Well, that's ridiculous. Doesn't he know all the balls you kept in the air at your church before?"

Daniel gave a half shrug. "In his mind, leading a small church isn't nearly as challenging as a church this size."

"You're not going to cut back, are you?" She felt annoyed and indignant about Chip's slight to Daniel's leadership and abilities. How could anyone think he wasn't up to the job?

"Not if I can help it. The Session meets on Friday. We'll talk about it then."

In a Presbyterian church, the Session—made up of the elders of the congregation—was the decision-making body for individual churches. A pastor's role was obviously one of authority, but they weren't the only or the final authority.

"Some of the programs have already been planned, right? The kids' pageant and the choir concert?"

"Yeah."

"Then you can't pull back on those at this point. It wouldn't be fair to the people who've been working on them. And you have to have the Christmas Eve service. What does he think you can cut?"

"I don't know. I really don't know what he's thinking."

Daniel looked discouraged, so she reached out to put a hand on his knee.

They sat in silence for a moment, but then she pulled her hand back when he shifted. "Eat your salad," she said, pushing the container toward him.

He made a face at her, but she gave him a steely glare so he obediently started to eat.

"Speaking of the choir," he said, "you should think about joining."

Her eyes widened. "Me? Why?"

"Because they can use some more members. I think you'd enjoy it."

"I can't be part of a choir."

"Why not? You've got a good voice." When she opened her mouth to object, he spoke over her. "I heard you. Remember? At the reception."

"Yeah, but…" She trailed off, mostly because she didn't have a good excuse.

"It might be good for you."

"Why would it be good for me?" She was starting to feel a familiar defensiveness. She didn't like the idea that Daniel might think she wasn't doing everything she needed to do as a pastor's wife, when she'd been going out of her way for the first couple of days to fill the role.

"Because you like to sing and you can contribute. And because you have a tendency to hide."

"I do not have a tendency to hide." Now she was feeling defensive for another reason. She hated it when he brought this topic up, and it didn't matter whether he was right or not. She hated the idea of having everyone stare at her and listen to her in the choir.

"Yeah, you do."

"I'm not a super-social person, but I don't hide. I talk to people plenty."

"So then the choir wouldn't be a big deal for you." He twitched his eyebrows at her in a way that was supposed to get her to smile.

She rolled her eyes at him instead of smiling.

"What's that look for?"

"That's for you being annoying."

He chuckled. "It was just a suggestion."

"Right."

"So are you going to do it or not?"

"I'll think about it."

"They practice on Wednesday evenings. Just for an hour."

"I said I'll think about it."

"Okay." He paused for a beat. "Do I get any of those cookies?"

She passed the bag to him, muttering, "Not that you deserve them."

Maybe Daniel thought she needed to be more involved in the church, participate in a lot of activities because she was married to him. Maybe the rest of the congregation expected it too, and he didn't want her to give them any reason to doubt he was a good fit. If she needed to, she would do it—whether she wanted to or not.

She was getting up to leave a little while later when Daniel said, "Oh, Martha said she was bringing by a casserole this afternoon."

"Why is she bringing a casserole?"

"Just being nice, I think."

"But why do we need a casserole? We're not sick or anything."

"What's the big deal? She's trying to be nice. I think they've arranged to bring us dinners all week."

"I'm perfectly capable of making something for dinner."

She actually *wasn't* perfectly capable of cooking dinner, but she was certainly planning to try. And it made her feel stupid and helpless that the ladies of the church had evidently decided she needed extra help—that she wasn't equipped to even be a normal wife, much less a pastor's wife.

"What are you so sensitive about? People are trying to be nice."

"I know." She bit back her initial response since she knew it was irrational, but it bothered her unduly.

She'd wanted a husband and family and now she had one, thanks to Daniel. She wasn't going to waste this opportunity. She was going to be a good wife, and in a traditional community like this, part of that role involved cooking dinner—at least some of the time. She couldn't even try if all the church ladies insisted on bringing over dinner.

She was still bothered when she went to spend the afternoon at her mother's nursing facility, working on her laptop while her mom dozed and then taking her outside for a walk when she was awake.

And she was still bothered when Martha came by late that afternoon with an entire delicious meal and stayed for an hour to chat and repeat the preparation directions six times.

The poppy seed chicken casserole, salad, rolls, and chocolate cake were wonderful, of course, and Jessica tried to feel grateful for it all as she and Daniel ate at the kitchen table that evening.

There were even leftovers for them to eat for lunch the next day.

She didn't feel as grateful as she should.

Jessica could be a decent pastor's wife. She was sure she could. If anyone would let her try.

She was about to suggest Daniel go with her on Bear's evening walk, but he disappeared outside to his workshop immediately after dinner.

He didn't come back in until bedtime.

Jessica took another shower before bed, and Daniel was reading again when she emerged.

But this time he didn't put his book down.

# FIVE

Jessica woke up trapped.

She gasped in surge of panic as she tried to move but couldn't. She was pinned in place.

As her mind gradually cleared from sleep, she realized it was Saturday morning, and she was imprisoned by the covers.

When she opened her eyes, she realized why.

Bear must have jumped on the bed sometime during the night. The dog was stretched out between Jessica and the edge of the bed, holding down the covers simply by lying on them.

Jessica wriggled until she'd created enough slack to turn over and then realized Daniel was holding down the other side. He'd rolled over so he was facing her, and somehow the covers had gotten tucked under his body.

Jessica squirmed some more, yanking the covers on Daniel's side since she groggily reasoned he'd be easier to move than the dog.

He huffed, shifted slightly, and clung to the covers.

She pulled even harder and freed them from his weight, the momentum of the pull causing him to roll over onto his back.

With a groan of relief, Jessica readjusted, giving herself more space by moving onto his side.

"Whassat," he mumbled, reaching out for her and pulling her to his side under the covers.

Jessica was perfectly amenable to this scenario, and she snuggled up against his warm, relaxed body.

"Y'okay?" he asked, fitting her against him, sounding barely more awake than he'd been before.

"Yeah. Just trapped by the covers." She wrapped an arm around his bare belly and let out a long exhale.

"Huh?"

"I was trapped between you and Bear."

"Oh." His hand stroked her hair, although he still seemed mostly asleep. "Sorry."

"Not your fault."

"Good. You feel nice."

She slanted her eyes up in surprise and saw that his eyes were still closed. "So do you."

"You feel nicer than me." He seemed to be almost smiling, although she had no idea how close he was to being awake.

She smiled back. "We'll have to agree to disagree about that."

He let out a thick exhale and pulled her closer, so she was practically lying on top of him. She felt him kiss her hair, and her heart melted a little in her chest.

Then he mumbled, "Wanted to hold you... like this... long time."

A surge of affection and excitement heightened the tenderness. She stroked his rough jaw, her cheek pressed against his chest. She was afraid to say anything—afraid he would wake up and wouldn't be so soft and clingy, afraid everything would change.

"Jessica," he murmured, still stroking her hair down her back.

"Hmm?" She shifted just slightly and realized he was hard. She could feel his arousal against her belly.

His hand slid down until he was cupping her bottom, pushing her weight against his groin. "Honey." The one word was almost a groan.

She moaned softly in response, growing aroused as much from the emotions she was feeling as from the feel of his hard body against hers. She squirmed against him, trying to generate deeper sensations.

He released a long, guttural sound, pressing her more tightly against him.

Then a loud clatter startled her so much she gasped.

Daniel jerked, jarred suddenly awake. "What was that?"

"Bear jumped off the bed," Jessica explained, her voice hoarse and a clench of disappointment in her gut.

He'd been half-asleep before. Things would be different now that he was fully awake. She knew it. She *knew* it. He'd be more like he'd been all this week.

"What was she doing on the bed?" He gave a soft groan as he pushed himself up to a sitting position, gently dislodging Jessica in the process.

"I don't know. She must have gotten cold or something and jumped up during the night."

"Okay." He rubbed his face urgently and glanced over at Jessica, who was flushed and sprawled out in the middle of the bed.

He looked away from her quickly, taking a strange, shuddering breath. "I better take a shower."

Jessica watched him walk, slightly stiffly, to the bathroom. Then she exhaled in resignation.

She glanced at the clock. It was just after five. A yummy interlude of sex was obviously not on the agenda this morning.

~

Jessica was ready early to go out to dinner so she sat on the edge of the bed near her nightstand and had a texted conversation with Kim.

She gave her friend some updates on the week and tried very hard not to whine about Daniel, which was what she really wanted to do.

The week had been okay—just not what Jessica had imagined when she'd envisioned herself married. Daniel had been friendly and considerate, but he'd spent most of the week at the church, in his study, or in the workshop. The women of the church brought them dinner every day—all of it far better than anything Jessica was capable of preparing herself. And they hadn't had sex. Not when they'd seemed close to it early this morning. Not at all.

Not since their wedding night. Exactly a week ago.

It was honestly rather annoying. She would never have expected them to have a week-long sexathon, but she'd assumed Daniel would want to have sex again, *sometime* during the week.

He hadn't mentioned it at all—not given her the slightest hint that he was interested, except for being hard that morning, which must have just been a physical response. She'd thought he'd enjoyed the one time they'd been together, but maybe it had just been a release after going so long without and it wasn't good enough to compel him to try it again anytime soon.

She tried not to brood on it. If she'd been more confident of her sexual abilities, she might have brought it up herself. But it was too new to her. She was too inexperienced. And she simply couldn't bring herself to ask for sex from a man who might not even be interested.

If she'd felt close to him in other ways, then going without sex wouldn't have been that big a deal. But no matter how nice he'd been this week, he'd still felt kind of distant. She couldn't exactly nail down what he was doing differently—other than spending a lot of time away from her—but she knew he was closing himself off. She didn't like it, but she wasn't sure what she could do about it.

She didn't want to complain. They didn't have a normal marriage, so she shouldn't expect him to hang out with her all the time. But she'd felt closer to him *before* they got married.

She didn't tell any of this to Kim though. She thought marriage issues should stay in the marriage, even in a strange, half marriage like she and Daniel had.

Daniel had been working in the yard most of the afternoon, cutting back overgrown tree branches and then working again in the workshop. About fifteen minutes earlier, she'd gone out to tell him he needed to start to get dressed or he wouldn't be ready when Will and Holly came to pick them up. He wouldn't let her into the workshop, and he wouldn't tell her when she asked what he was working on.

He just said, "I've got a few different projects going on," which was a very annoying nonanswer.

He'd rushed through a shower and now emerged from the bathroom wearing only a pair of black trousers.

His broad shoulders, fine chest, flat stomach, and lean hips made her gulp.

"Who are you texting?" he asked.

"Kim." She wrote out one last text and set the phone down.

"How's she doing?"

"Fine. Still dating that guy."

"How's it going?" He spoke through the fabric of the T-shirt he was pulling on over his head.

"Okay, I guess. She's not really sure what he's thinking. About the relationship, I mean."

"It's not a good sign when the woman doesn't know what the man is thinking. If he's really serious about it, she would know."

Jessica tried very hard not to roll her eyes. "Should I tell her that?"

He raised his eyebrows at her slightly snide tone. "No. I was just saying." He picked up a gray dress shirt from the bed where he'd thrown it earlier and pulled it on over his shoulders. "Is everything all right with you?"

His dark eyes were questioning, slightly concerned.

"Yes. Of course. Why wouldn't it be?" Her tone was supposed to be calm and reasonable, but she didn't quite pull it off. She just couldn't get rid of her bad mood.

He didn't pursue the subject, which was probably a good thing since she might have snapped his head off if he had.

He was tucking in his shirt when he asked, "How has your mom been this week?"

Jessica really didn't need to think about that. She gave a faint shrug.

"Not good?"

She shook her head. "I thought having me close so I could see her every day would help, but it was a really bad week. She didn't know who I was today. Even in the morning."

Despite her best efforts, her voice cracked on the last word.

"Why didn't you tell me?"

She gave another shrug, managing not to mutter that he hadn't bothered to ask.

Jessica felt a little like crying, but she wasn't going to do it. For one thing, she'd actually put on a little mascara for the evening, and she wasn't going to mess it up.

"I'm sorry about your mom," he said, genuine sympathy in his tone. He slid on a belt as he spoke. "I'm sorry I didn't ask about her before."

"It's fine. You don't have to ask about her. I'll tell you if anything important happens."

She didn't want him to do anything for her out of obligation. She only wanted what he wanted to give her.

Which evidently wasn't much.

She shook her head slightly, brushing off the unfair thought. He hadn't done anything wrong. She was the one who'd had unrealistic expectations about what marriage would be like and so was disappointed that hers wasn't living up to them. It wasn't right to take her disappointment out on Daniel.

"Your mom has had some bad spells before, right, and she's bounced back?"

"Yeah. But eventually she isn't going to bounce back."

This might be the time her mom wasn't going to bounce back. The thought caused a sickening clench in her gut.

Bear came loping into the room just then. She'd been gobbling up her dinner in the kitchen but must have finished and come to find her people. She walked over to the bed, and Jessica bent over to pet her, taking comfort as always in the soft hair and the adoring eyes.

When she looked up at Daniel, she saw he was standing perfectly still, one arm in the jacket he'd been pulling on, and he was gazing at her steadily.

It was impossible to miss the expression of empathy in his eyes.

Jessica wiped at her eye before the tear fell. "I'm fine. Maybe she'll be better next week."

She cleared her throat and was relieved when he broke the gaze and pulled his jacket all the way on.

She absently wiped a white hair from Bear off her good black pants. They were having dinner tonight with a couple from the church, and it was at a fancy restaurant in a larger city about forty minutes away. It was a kind of Christmas gift from the couple to her and Daniel.

Jessica would much rather have gotten a gift card. Dressing up and going out to eat was the last thing she wanted to do after the week she'd had. She'd been planning to try to cook dinner herself since a church lady had brought over an egg casserole and fruit salad for breakfast, which meant they were on their own for dinner.

But instead she had to go out—and sit in the backseat of someone else's car for forty minutes there and back to get there.

She knew Holly—who worked in a department store a couple of towns over—would be dressed to the nines, but Jessica was feeling so blah today that she couldn't muster the energy to wear a skirt. So she'd worn her black pants with a black silk shell that was made to look like it laced up the front and a wine-colored cardigan that looked a little festive.

When she glanced over at Daniel, he was putting on his watch. "You can't wear that jacket," she said, noticing something immediately.

He glanced down. "Why not?"

"It's got a stain on it."

"It's black."

"Even so." She walked over and pointed out the obvious stain just under the pocket.

The jacket was getting pretty old anyway. He'd been wearing it for years—since well before Lila died.

Almost every piece of clothing he owned had been picked out by Lila. She couldn't remember the last time she'd seen him in something new.

He made a grumbling sound under his breath, but he took the jacket off. "Do you think I'll be okay without a jacket?"

"I don't know. It's a pretty snotty place. They might try to give you one before they let you in." She went to look at his clothes in the closet.

"I've got that old corduroy—"

"No. You can't wear that." She sorted through his collection of jackets—most of which were looking rather rough. He still had decent suits for Sunday, but not much else.

"I don't really want to wear a suit," he said, coming to stand beside her and inspect his wardrobe.

"Here," she said, finding a perfectly fine black jacket in the back of the closet.

"The button fell off." He pulled the button out of the pocket, where he'd obviously put it before he'd stuffed the jacket at the back of the closet.

She shook her head. "There's a fairly simple solution to that dilemma."

She wasn't crafty or domestic at all. She didn't sew or embroider or any of the old-fashioned skills that many women still mastered in Willow Park.

But she could at least manage to sew on a button.

"We don't have time," he said, when she found a little needle and thread kit in one of her dresser drawers.

"It will take two minutes. Your choices are to wait for the button or wear a suit."

He sighed and lowered himself to the side of the bed to put on his socks.

As he did, Bear walked over to greet him since she innocently assumed he'd come down to her level for that very reason.

Jessica watched from the corner of her eye as she hurriedly tacked on the button. Bear kept nosing at Daniel, confused that he wasn't responding.

She tried not to get annoyed about his ignoring her sweet dog.

"Have you thought any more about the choir?" he asked, as he slid on his shoe.

She'd hoped he'd forgotten about that idea. "I've thought a little about it."

"And?"

"I'm still thinking."

"That means you want to say no."

"Yes, I want to say no. You know that was my first inclination."

"I thought you were serious about thinking about it." His tone had changed, evidently in response to the testiness in her tone.

"I *was* serious about thinking about it. But thinking about it doesn't automatically mean I'm going to come down on your side. Believe it or not, your opinion isn't the only reasonable conclusion for every issue in the universe."

He narrowed his eyes. "That's ridiculous. And I'm not sure you've even thought about it. You're just stalling and hoping I'll let it go."

The fact that he was right did nothing to ease her annoyance with him. "Do you have any idea how arrogant you sound—assuming you know exactly what I'm thinking? You have no idea what's going on in my mind."

"So what *is* going on in your mind?" Bear was concerned about the rising temper in the room and nuzzled at Daniel's legs again. He nudged her away, appearing unconscious of what he was doing since he was entirely focused on the conversation.

"I don't have to tell you everything I'm thinking." She'd finished the button so she tossed the jacket toward him on the bed. She got up, returned the kit to the drawer, and then closed it a little harder than necessary. "You certainly don't tell me."

"What is that supposed to mean?" He pushed Bear away again.

"She wants you to say hi to her," Jessica burst out. "Is even *that* too much to ask?"

His eyes widened in obvious surprise, but he leaned over to pat the dog's head. Evidently satisfied in getting a greeting, Bear ambled over to Jessica again.

"What do you mean by 'even that'?" Daniel asked, a different resonance in his tone.

She knew exactly what he was asking, but she didn't know how to answer the question, so she acted confused. "What?"

"You said 'even *that*' is too much to ask, like you've asked more of me and I haven't delivered."

"I didn't mean it like that. Don't get hung up on a random comment."

He was peering at her in a way she didn't like at all—like he might see things he wasn't supposed to see.

Jessica just wanted the whole discussion to be over. It was irrational and futile and accomplishing nothing. "We should get going. They'll be over here to pick us up any minute."

"Yeah." He was still looking at her, but he leaned down to brush a few white dog hairs off his pants. He was frowning as he did.

For some reason, the gesture made Jessica mad. She glared at him and then went to her closet to grab an old-fashioned lint brush that used to be her mother's. Making sure she turned it the right away, she leaned over to brush off his trousers.

"If you don't want her hair on your pants, then you can just keep pushing her away," Jessica muttered.

"What has gotten into you?" he demanded. He took the brush from her hand and took her by one arm to straighten her up.

"Nothing. Bear is important to me."

"I know she is. I've never said a word about her, except she should sleep on her own bed."

"I know you've never liked her."

"I like her fine. I just don't like her as much as you do. She's your dog, after all."

"I know that."

"Then why are you in a snit about this?"

He couldn't have chosen a word more poised to rile her up if he'd tried. "I am not in a snit," she gritted out.

"You are too in a snit. I've been trying to have a normal conversation here, and you're acting like everything I do and say is a source of resentment."

He was right. *Of course* he was right. But the fact that he had no idea why she might be upset—why she might have wanted more from this marriage—just made her feel even worse.

She'd made a mess of this whole thing. She needed to pull it together and not expect more than he wanted to give her.

His arm tightened slightly on her upper arm. "Would you just tell me what's wrong with you? You don't have to come tonight if you don't want."

"Of course I'm going to come tonight. What do you think I'll do? Tell Will and Holly that I don't feel like going out, so I'm sending my husband to have dinner with them alone? Give me a little credit."

"Then what the—"

His frustrated question was interrupted by the ringing of their front door.

Bear barked excitedly, and Jessica grabbed her purse, relieved at the narrow escape.

"Don't forget your jacket," she told him.

∼

Will drove them in his expensive SUV, and Jessica spent the entire ride to the restaurant trying to be friendly and make casual conversation.

Since Holly was a talker, she dominated the conversation, so fortunately Jessica didn't have to interact with Daniel very much. She was still rattled and upset by their interrupted argument, and whenever she didn't have to talk, she kept trying to talk her emotions back into order.

She was usually a very calm and sensible person. There was no reason to get so uptight about everything. Eventually, she and Daniel would work out a relationship that was good for both of them. He was allowed to be a little distant in the first week.

She didn't look at him very much during the car ride, afraid he'd read something in her expression. Instead, she stared outside at the winter evening and the Christmas decorations—some of them crazy over-the-top. She tried to work up some Christmas spirit, thinking that she would be married for the Christmas season for the first time in her life.

She didn't manage to summon up very much enthusiasm.

They finally got to the restaurant, which was just as exclusive and snobby as she remembered. The food was ludicrously expensive, and she couldn't help but think this couple was rather pretentious and thoughtless to invite them here on a Saturday night.

Daniel needed to preach tomorrow morning, after all. They'd be really late getting home tonight.

There were a few teetotalers in the congregation, but not many, and Will and Holly weren't among them. So they had a bottle of red wine and chatted over four courses of food.

Daniel was his normal charming self, but she could tell he was still wondering what was wrong with her. He would occasionally watch her questioningly. She started to wonder if maybe he thought she'd make a scene at the restaurant and embarrass him, although that thought was probably unfair too.

But just because she knew her attitude toward him this evening was unfair didn't mean it was easy to get rid of.

She hoped the tension wasn't obvious to the other couple.

Over coffee, she excused herself since she needed to use the restroom before the long ride home. On her way back the table, she ran into someone she knew.

"Hey, Mike," she said, smiling as he stopped. "What are you doing here?"

Mike was about her age and cute in a nerdy way, with dark-rimmed glasses and an adorably crooked smile. He'd worked with her for a couple of years before he'd gotten another job, and she was happy to see him.

"Having dinner. I live in Dalton." He hugged her casually and was smiling when he pulled away. "What are you doing here?"

"I'd forgotten you lived here now. I've moved back to Willow Park."

They chatted for a few minutes, getting updates on their lives. He was a really nice guy—smart and funny. He'd hit on her the first time they'd met, but he'd been good-natured when she'd turned him down flat—since she only dated guys who shared her religious beliefs. He was showing her a project he was working on, both of them huddled over his smart phone to look at the screen he'd pulled up, when a voice behind her made her jump.

"There you are."

She turned around in surprise and saw Daniel, watching them coolly.

"Oh, hi. Sorry." She glanced at her watch, embarrassed that she'd lost track of time. "I didn't realize I was gone so long. I ran into Mike."

Daniel's shoulders had stiffened, and he stepped over to stand beside her, putting his hand on her back. Despite the gesture, he didn't feel friendly and affectionate. He felt uncharacteristically tense. She had no idea what was wrong with him.

"Mike does web development too," Jessica told him. "We used to work together." She turned to Mike. "This is my husband, Daniel."

"It's great to meet you." Mike extended his hand with a smile, looking genuinely friendly.

Daniel looked anything but friendly as he returned the handshake.

"Will and Holly are waiting for us." He nodded toward the front entrance. "They were worried you were taking so long."

"Oh. Sorry." She squeezed Mike's arm and told him good-bye and then returned the hug he gave her. She was aware of Daniel's steady gaze on her as she did.

She frowned as she walked down the hall with him. She kept slanting him looks to confirm, but he definitely looked angry. Cold and angry, not the familiar grumpiness she was more used to from him.

"What's wrong with you?" she asked at last, stopping in the middle of the hall.

"Nothing." He put a hand in the middle of her back and pushed her forward, but she resisted the gesture.

"Why are you angry?"

"I'm not angry." He made a quick gesture of his head, like he was trying to rid himself of his mood. "Sorry."

"Don't be sorry. Just tell me what's wrong. Are you upset that I took so long? I didn't mean to be rude, but if you think Holly and—"

"No, no. It's nothing like that." His hard expression broke. "I'm sorry. I'm just being stupid. You can talk to whoever you want, whenever you want."

He sounded more natural now, having worked through whatever bothered him. But she still wanted to know what it was. "Why wouldn't I be able to... Wait, were you mad that was talking to *Mike*?" She'd belatedly landed on an explanation for his inexplicable mood.

"I wasn't mad. But it's clear that he's into you, and it's just unsettling for a man to walk into a hall and find another man coming on to his wife."

She choked, half on indignation that he would trust her so little—that he'd think she might respond to another man when she was married to him—and half on laughter, at how crazy the idea actually was.

There was not another man in the world that she wanted the way she wanted Daniel. She'd never fully admitted it to herself before, but there it was…

She had no idea how to respond, and fortunately she didn't have time to say anything anyway. They'd reached Will and Holly, and Daniel said, "I found her."

Jessica apologized for taking so long, and they all got into the car.

Daniel still felt kind of tense beside her, and she wondered if he'd really thought she was flirting with Mike.

She didn't know how to flirt. She'd never been able to master the skill.

If she'd known how, she would have tried it on Daniel a long time ago.

~

Holly was the only one still in a talking mood on the way back to Willow Park.

Daniel kept up his end of the conversation, but Jessica was just too tired and distracted.

She leaned her head back against the seat and closed her eyes for a few seconds, wondering what she'd gotten herself into.

Married to this frustrating, incomprehensible man. Till death did them part.

The next thing she knew, the car was coming to a stop. She jerked awake, completely disoriented.

She was leaning her head against a shoulder, and her face was pressed against a black jacket.

She blinked and saw through the front windshield of the SUV they were stopped at one of the three traffic lights in Willow Park.

She straightened up with a jerk, embarrassed that she'd actually fallen asleep. She couldn't help but glance up at Daniel. He was gazing at her in the dim light.

She couldn't read his expression, but he didn't look cold and angry anymore.

"I'm sorry," she said, speaking to Will and Holly in the front seats. "I can't believe I fell asleep. You must think I'm incredibly rude."

"Oh, no," Holly said, a smile in her voice. "Please don't worry about it. It's late, and Daniel said you'd had a really long week."

Jessica glanced over at him in surprise, but his expression was no more revealing than before.

~

That night, Daniel didn't read in bed. He turned off his bedside light as soon as she crawled under the covers beside him

He was looking at her in the dark, so she turned to face him.

"I'm sorry about before," he said. "I shouldn't have gotten angry. Or jealous. Or any of it, really."

She let out a gusty breath, relieved the strange tension could be over now. "I'm sorry too. I got angry first. I... I shouldn't have taken out my frustration on you."

"Can you tell me *why* you were frustrated?"

She should have seen the trap coming from miles away, but she hadn't. She wasn't prepared. She just looked at him silently, any words she might have said frozen in her throat.

"I know I'm sometimes clueless, but I don't think I'm wrong about this. It's like you're really upset and annoyed with me but won't tell me why."

She let out a breath. "Yeah."

"So can you please tell me? I can't fix it if you won't let me know why you're unhappy."

"There's nothing to fix," she said at last, her voice a little hoarse. "It's not like you've really done anything wrong. And I don't want you to feel guilty or anything, or be obliged to act in any way you don't want."

She could barely see him frowning in the dark. "I don't know what you mean."

"I know you don't. I know." She blew out a frustrated breath, wishing she'd just kept her mouth closed to avoid this awkward conversation. She pulled the covers up over her, causing him to adjust the covers over himself too. "It's just that... it's just that before we got married, I thought we were close."

"We *are* close."

"I know. I *know*. But it felt different before. We were honest with each other and basically open about what was going on with us, and we spent time together. And now that we're married, we... we don't. We aren't." She took a shuddering breath, afraid of saying too much. "And I've been kind of upset about it. Since it feels like we're not even as close as we used to be."

"We're still clos—" He broke off his initial response, as if he'd just processed what she said.

"We haven't been close this week. I mean, you're always very nice, but you've... you seem withdrawn, and I don't know why. I don't know what I've done to make you pull away from me." She felt painfully vulnerable saying the words and wished she could suck them back up.

He rolled over onto his back and stared at the ceiling. A faint glow from the moonlight played around the edges of the blinds on the windows, casting dim light across his face. "You haven't done anything."

"Then why..." She didn't finish the question. She didn't need to.

He didn't answer immediately. Just shifted slightly beneath the covers. Then eventually he said, "It's hard. Harder than I thought. Getting married again."

Her chest suddenly clamped down in pain at the halted explanation. What an absolute, insensitive idiot she'd been—not to realize that he might be struggling with something really difficult.

"It feels like I'm moving on," he said. "Even if I can't let... Even if it's not the same, I've started doing things with you that I've never done with anyone but Lila. And not just the sex."

It hurt the way it had the first time, to hear him once again affirm that he was never going to fall in love with her, but she already knew that was true so she pushed it aside in the face of what was so much more important.

"I understand," she murmured, reaching out to put a hand on his chest. "I'm so sorry. I never even realized... I'm so sorry."

"Don't be sorry. It's not your fault. I know I shouldn't feel guilty for moving on, but I do. Sometimes I do." Emotion was shuddering under the surface of his composure, so intensely it seemed to vibrate the air around him. "I didn't realize it would be so hard."

Her eyes burned with feeling. "It's okay, Daniel. It's really okay. I shouldn't have tried to push you—"

"You didn't push me at all. I should have told you what was wrong. I've been trying to be a good husband to you—I really have—but I haven't done a good job this week."

She couldn't resist anymore, so she rolled over to give him a hug.

He hugged her back, so tightly she couldn't breathe for a moment.

Then he murmured into her hair, "I'll try to do better."

"You don't have to do better—"

"I do. I don't want you to be unhappy. It's my responsibility to make sure you aren't. And I don't want you to ever doubt that we're friends, that we're close. You mean so much to me, Jessica."

She didn't doubt it anymore. He felt real and warm and human beneath her, strong and vulnerable both.

He added, "And if you're upset about something, would you try to let me know what it is earlier too?"

"Yeah. Sorry. I didn't want to grumble since it's not a real marriage. I mean, a regular marriage. You don't owe me anything."

"I owe you being a good husband, and I'm sorry I haven't been that."

"I'm sorry too."

She felt a lot better, and she didn't want to move out of his arms, so she shifted against him, getting a little more comfortable.

He didn't seem inclined to push her away tonight, so she stretched out against his side, her arm wrapped around his waist.

As the minutes past, she started thinking more and more about sex. He was so big. And strong. And solid. And hot. She wanted to feel him in every way.

But she was determined not to put any pressure on him. Not if it made him feel guilty. Not if he wasn't ready. There was no reason to be selfish, just because her body had ideas of its own.

She kept shifting, however, since her body was responding to thoughts she shouldn't be having. She tried to keep her hand still, but it was moving slightly against his side—quite against her conscious volition.

Without thinking, she moved her hand down to his hip, past the waistband of his pajama pants. She wasn't doing anything intentional, just idly stroking her fingers.

Then her forearm brushed against something unexpected.

She sucked in a breath and couldn't help but move her hand down to investigate.

He was aroused. It was obvious beneath the fabric of his pants.

"Jessica," he said, his voice very thick. She gave a ragged gasp as she gently palmed him, thrilled with how he felt beneath her hand.

She jerked away when she realized what she was doing. "I'm so sorry. I'm so *sorry*. We don't have to do anything you're not ready for. I shouldn't have—"

Horribly guilty and horribly embarrassed, she rolled over to her side of the bed and pulled the covers up to her neck.

He rolled over toward her, dislodging the safety of her covers.

"Jessica," he said, taking her face in his hand, "I'd like to have sex again, if you want to."

"But I thought you said—"

"I've been feeling guilty, but it's not a rational feeling and I shouldn't indulge it. I think it's better for me to… I'd like to have sex again, if you'd like to too."

"I would," she admitted, reaching up to slide her fingers through his hair.

He leaned down to kiss her, and it was just as good as last time. His tongue slowly explored her mouth until she was shuddering with pleasure. She stroked his cheek, loving the feel of his beard beneath her palm.

It didn't take long until both of them were completely into it. She was even more eager than last time—so eager, in fact, that she came once during foreplay, a fact that seemed to please Daniel inordinately.

When he slid inside her again, he was just as hot and hard and urgent as he'd been the week before.

He seemed to try to control his rhythm, slow his motion inside her, but he couldn't. Soon he was grunting with the same kind of primal need she'd felt in him last time.

She loved how it felt, loved how he so obviously took pleasure in her body, how he seemed to need what she could offer him.

She didn't climax from intercourse, but after he'd come with a loud exclamation of release, he kissed her some more and brought her to another orgasm with his fingers.

She was limp and replete when he finally collapsed beside her with a long, low groan.

She couldn't help but smile at how exhausted he sounded.

"Surely having sex with me isn't such an arduous task," she teased.

He reached over to pull her to his side. "It's exhausting. You're quite the taskmaster."

She giggled foolishly. "Well, you performed admirably."

"Glad to hear it." He leaned down to press a kiss into her hair. "Are you sore?"

"Not nearly as much this time."

"Good."

She eventually got up to go to the bathroom and make sure Bear was sleeping soundly.

When she came back to bed, she rolled back over to his side and fell asleep very happy.

# SIX

The following week, she was determined to do better—to enjoy what she was getting out of this marriage and not hope for or expect anything more.

She'd always had a certain idea about what a home would feel like after she was married, and there was no reason why she couldn't cultivate some of those feelings—whether Daniel was in love with her or not.

Her first step toward this end was to cook dinner on Monday evening. In all her visions of herself as a wife, she would at least sometimes make meals other than canned soup and sandwiches.

They'd had a potluck at church on Sunday evening after the final practice for the children's Christmas pageant, and she wasn't about to bring something she tried cooking for the first time to be tasted by half the church. So she brought fruit salad to the potluck. No one seemed surprised that she hadn't tried anything more ambitious, but she was determined to eventually do more than people expected of her.

She spent all of Sunday and half of Monday mulling over what she would to try to cook on Monday evening.

She finally settled on a roast since she remembered how tasty and homey it had been when her mother cooked them. It felt like an impressive meal, but the recipes she found looked doable. She went to the grocery store on Monday morning to buy a good piece of meat and all the vegetables and seasonings she needed. She took a long, late lunch break to get it all prepared. She followed the directions exactly and double-checked every step.

She used the simplest recipe she found, and she was sure she'd done everything correctly as she put it in the oven.

She was excited. Ridiculously proud of herself. It might not be as easy for her as for other women, but she could prepare a home-cooked dinner for her husband just like any other wife in Willow Park.

It started to smell good as it got closer to dinnertime. Bear planted herself in the middle of the kitchen to wait. The dog had never smelled a piece of meat being cooked in her house for such a long stretch of time, so it absorbed her attention for the entire afternoon.

Jessica brought her laptop into the kitchen and worked on some stuff that didn't require the entire computer setup in her office. She'd always been good at tuning the world out as she worked. It was one of her gifts, and it came in very handy as she worked from home.

Her supervisor had just sent her a new project, so she started making plans—the bare bones of the design and the timeline.

Eventually, she became aware that Bear had started to pace the length of the kitchen.

"Lie down," she said distractedly, typing as quickly as she could.

The dog didn't lie down.

"Bear, sit."

Bear sat, but then popped up again less than a minute later.

"What's wrong with you?" Jessica groaned, finally turning toward the dog, who was now standing frozen and pointing toward the oven.

Jessica gasped and leapt out of her chair. It was past time for the roast to come out. Daniel would be home any minute.

"Shit!" She ran toward the oven and grabbing the hot pads she'd put on the counter earlier in the day when she'd been careful about every detail.

She opened the oven, coughing at the wave of heat that rushed out at her. Ignoring it, she grabbed the big pan and dragged it out, coughing more as she did.

"Shit, shit, shit, shit, shit." She gasped, grabbing the first utensil she could lay her hands on. It happened to be a big wooden spoon.

She poked the piece of meat. It didn't look burnt. She was only ten minutes late in taking it out. Surely it wasn't entirely ruined. She calmed down at this logical conclusion, although she was surprised and disturbed that the expensive roast had ended up half the size it had been when she'd put it in.

Poking the meat with the spoon produced no verifiable results.

She pushed the meat too hard with the spoon and the pan started to slide. She reached out to hold it steady, burning her fingers in the process. "Shit!"

"What on earth is the matter?"

She whirled around, sucking on her burned fingers and holding the wooden spoon up like a wand.

Daniel stood in the kitchen, staring at her in astonishment. He wore khakis and a green dress shirt, and his lips were slightly parted.

He looked scrumptious, and she was a perfect mess.

"Nothing," she managed to say. "I might have overcooked the roast a little."

He came over to investigate. "It sounded like the house was falling down."

"Yeah. Sorry about the language."

"It's fine. Are you sure everything is all right?"

"Yeah. I was just all in a rush when I took it out of the oven, and I burned my fingers. I don't usually use that kind of language."

"I said it's fine." He frowned at her. "Do you really think I judge everything you do? There's nothing in the Bible that says you can't use the word 'shit.' Believe it or not, occasionally I do too."

"You do?" She forgot her roast momentarily in genuine curiosity. "I've never heard you say it."

"It offends some people, so I try not to use it in public." He came over to stand beside her near the counter. His frown had turned into a familiar half smile. "But you know, sometimes things really *are* shit, and there's no other appropriate word to describe it."

She smiled at him sheepishly, then turned back toward her roast. "Let's hope this isn't one of those times when there's no other appropriate word."

"I'm sure it's fine." He peered at the concoction in the pan and pointed out a pale, gelatinous mass. "What's that?"

"It's a potato." The vegetables hadn't fared well for some reason, but most of them looked edible.

"Are you sure?"

She groaned at his dubious tone. "Well, it was. I thought I did everything right. Surely ten extra minutes wouldn't ruin the entire thing!"

He started to chuckle but clearly bit back the instinct. "I'm sure it's fine. I don't mind well-done meat. Do I have time to change clothes?"

"Yeah. I'll get everything ready. I've got to try to cut this thing up." She prayed the meat would taste good. It smelled pretty good, and it didn't look too bad.

"I don't mind carving the—"

"I can do it. You go change clothes."

She moved all her work stuff, telling herself that next time she was definitely going to set the oven timer. Why the heck hadn't she thought of that before? Then she set the table with the dishes they'd received as wedding gifts.

She lit a candle—not tapers, just a big chunky one that had been sitting on the counter. Then she cut the meat, which was tougher than she'd been hoping. She hadn't eaten a roast like this in a long time, but she was sure it was tougher than it was supposed to be.

She covered the meat with au jus, hoping the gravy would soak up and soften it. Then she spooned the vegetables into a bowl, cringing when a couple of the potatoes broke into mush.

So it wasn't perfect. But maybe it would taste okay.

She put it all on the table and then decided the candle might be silly so she started to blow it out.

"It looks great," Daniel said, entering the kitchen wearing a T-shirt and a much more beat-up pair of khakis.

She didn't blow out the candle after all since he'd already seen it. She didn't think the meal looked great, but he was obviously trying to be nice.

He said the blessing, and she served the food, intentionally giving him the potatoes that appeared to have the most internal consistency.

She sipped her water and watched out of the corner of her eye as he took his first bite.

His face didn't transform with disgust, so maybe it was edible.

She watched as he chewed. And chewed. And chewed. And chewed.

Then she groaned in defeat and lowered her head to the table. "It's horrible! You don't have to eat it."

He finally managed to swallow, although it seemed to take some effort. "It's fine."

"No, it's not. It's nice of you to pretend, but there's no sense in forcing yourself to eat this mess." With a sigh, she stirred her meat around with her fork. "I don't know what I did wrong. Maybe ten extra minutes was just too long."

"Or maybe it was just a bad cut of meat," he said, peering at the roast on the platter. "It probably wasn't your fault."

"It sure cost a lot to be a bad cut of meat." She cringed at how much she'd paid for it.

All she'd wanted to do is cook a decent meal and prove she was capable of being a pastor's wife.

"Then maybe it wasn't a good recipe you used—maybe it had you set the temperature too high or something."

His voice was casual and friendly, but he was peering at her face in concern.

She thought it was sweet he was trying to take the blame off her, but it also made her feel even more stupid. "I wonder what I did wrong."

"I don't know anything about roast. All I can do is grill stuff outside. Lila always cooked roast in the slow cooker."

It probably always turned out perfectly too. "I can ask my mom if she's lucid tomorrow. Sometimes she can remember things like recipes."

"If not, just ask someone at church—Martha or Rebecca or someone. I'm sure they'd be able to help."

There was no way Jessica was going to ask one of the women at church about why her roast had been a disaster, but she didn't say so to Daniel. She stood up and picked up both of their plates. "I'll make us sandwiches."

He helped her by carrying the bowl of vegetables and platter of meat to the counter.

He peered at her face closely. "Are you upset? Anyone could have ended up with a bad roast."

"But *I'm* the only one who did it. I'd tried so hard—" She broke off since she didn't want Daniel to know how much time and effort she'd spent preparing this meal.

He didn't respond immediately. Just stood a little too close to her near the counter. "It was nice of you to make it. I thought you didn't like to cook."

"I don't. I mean, I don't mind it—I just don't know how to do anything. I was trying."

She felt stupid and young and incompetent and a complete disaster as a wife.

She turned away from him—toward the sink to clean out the plates—as she gasped on a ludicrous wave of emotion, one that completely surprised her.

"Hey," he said, turning her around with a hand on her shoulder. "I don't care if you can cook or not. You don't ever have to cook for me."

"I know. But *I* care."

"Well, it was a good effort." He turned toward the very tough meat.

His face was perfectly sober, but she could see just the smallest hint of a repressed smile, as though he were hiding amusement.

"You can laugh."

"I don't want to laugh."

"Yes, you do. It's ridiculous. You can laugh."

He frowned at her in annoyance. "I'm not going to laugh when you're upset."

Suddenly, she was hit by a wave of amusement—at how she'd gotten so worked up over something so inconsequential, at his valiant attempt to say the right thing, and at the pitiful outcome of all her meal preparations.

What was happening to her? Just six months ago, she'd never dreamed she would get so upset over failing to cook a meal successfully. Most of her life, she'd barely even tried to cook, but she thought it was something a pastor's wife should be able to do.

Daniel smiled and looked visibly relieved when he saw her shift of mood. "Let's not have sandwiches," he said. "I'll take you out for dinner."

"Okay." She wiped her eyes, feeling better over the whole thing.

"I'll clear this up. Did you want to change clothes?"

She glanced down at herself. She'd been so intent on the meal that she hadn't even thought about putting on something decent or looking somewhat attractive. She wore sweats, a T-shirt, and no bra.

"Yeah. I'd better. You can just leave it. I can clean up later."

"Okay."

She went upstairs and pulled on jeans and a decent top. She ran a brush through her hair and was ready to go in about three minutes.

As she came down, Daniel was cleaning up—despite her clear instructions not to.

She was about to chastise him as she stood in the entrance of the kitchen, watching him dump the ruined food in the trash.

Before she could speak though, she saw him pick out a big piece of meat.

He passed it down to Bear, who was begging just at his heel.

"Shh," he told the dog, raising a finger to his lips. "Don't tell."

Bear, chomping happily on her meat, did as she was instructed and didn't say a word.

~

Cooking dinner hadn't turned out exactly as she'd planned it, but she wasn't prepared to give up on her goal of pursuing the kind of home experience she'd always envisioned. Her next step toward achieving that goal was to have a festive, cozy time decorating the Christmas tree with Daniel.

She'd always imagined families—bigger families than her and her mom—having warm, joyous times trimming the tree, filled with laughter and intimacy. She'd always wanted that for herself.

That Wednesday evening was the children's Christmas pageant. The program was just an hour, however, and she and Daniel agreed to decorate their tree after the pageant.

Jessica was very excited.

She'd always gotten a tree for her little house in Charlotte, but she'd had to decorate it by herself. One year she'd invited friends over to do it with her, but it hadn't been the experience she was hoping for. She thought this evening would be different.

Daniel had to stay at church longer than she did to talk to someone after the pageant, so she came home and got everything ready.

She made hot cider and got out the Christmas cookies she'd made that afternoon—the cookies were from preprepared dough, and she'd sat vigilantly in front of the oven so she wouldn't burn them. Then she put on Christmas music and pulled out the boxes of ornaments both of them had collected over the years.

A church member had given them the tree, and it was a really good Fraser fir they'd set up in the living room near the fireplace.

When everything was prepared, she waited impatiently for Daniel to get back. The living room was cozy, and the evening was cold. With the festive music and all the ornaments surrounding her, it really felt like the holidays.

Daniel came in a few minutes later. He wore black trousers and a dress shirt since he always wore something decent for church events. He grinned at her as he walked in and reached down to grab four of the cookies as soon as he saw them.

He ate them all, one after the other. They were obviously good since he didn't have to make a pretend face of enjoying them.

She laughed and shook her head at his appetite. "Do you want to change clothes?"

"Nah. No need. I don't think it should take too long to get this done."

Well, that wasn't too promising. She'd been hoping they could make a whole evening out of it—really spend time together and enjoy the holiday spirit.

She told herself not to be disappointed since he clearly didn't know she'd built up the evening in her mind. "Okay," she said casually. "Just don't blame me if you get glitter on your pretty shirt."

He glanced down at his French blue shirt. "Pretty?"

She giggled at his expression and got up to grab the lights.

Everything went smoothly. They didn't squabble or get bogged down in annoyances. Nothing awkward or tense occurred. Daniel was kind of quiet though.

She tried to think of funny things to talk about, thinking he might be hit by poignant memories of decorating Christmas trees with Lila, and he started to smile more.

Pleased he was warming up, Jessica's excitement built up again, but then his phone rang. He glanced at the screen before he took it.

She could tell something had happened just by the tone of his voice.

She resigned herself to the end of the evening when he said, "I'll be over there as soon as I can."

When he hung up, she gave him a questioning look.

"Paul Hanson had a heart attack."

"Oh no," she gasped, forgetting her own disappointment. "Is he all right?"

"He's still alive. They've taken him to the hospital. I should get over there."

"Of course. Leave right now. Do you want me to go with you?"

"No. There's nothing for you to do, so you might as well stay here and finish this up."

She blinked. "Oh. We can do it later—"

"No. It's fine. You finish up. I'm not sure what time I'll be back."

"Okay. Call and let me know how he is, and let me know if I can do anything for Rachel."

He left, and Jessica slumped to the couch, looking at the partly decorated tree.

It was fine. This was part of being a pastor. You got called at any hour of the day when an emergency happened to someone in your congregation.

Daniel didn't have a choice, and she certainly didn't begrudge his responsibilities.

It would have been nice if he'd wanted her to wait so he could finish decorating the tree with her, but that was no big deal.

She might be married, but that didn't mean she would have warm, happy holiday evenings.

She really should know better by now.

∼

The next day Paul was doing better—still in the hospital but evidently not about to die.

Jessica worked all day, and Daniel spent some time at the hospital and the rest of the time in his office. In the evening, he had a new member's class at the church which had dinner as part of it, so she didn't even get to have dinner with him.

She decided to have a nice evening by herself. Even if she couldn't hang out with him, she could enjoy a cozy time on her own with just Bear for company. She'd lived many years by herself, and she didn't need a man to enjoy an evening.

She straightened the room up and turned on the lights on the Christmas tree. She was settling down to read, but then decided to build a fire. A church member had brought over a load of firewood for them, so she brought some logs inside.

She knew how to build a fire. Her mom had made them all the time when she was a girl. So she set up the logs and then lit the fire without any sort of problem.

It started easily, and the fire soon blazed merrily.

It made the room cozy and festive, especially with the lit tree.

She was very pleased with the result, and she stretched out on the couch to read with some cocoa. After a while, she coughed a few times but didn't immediately notice what was making her cough.

On her fourth cough, she put down her e-reader.

Something was wrong.

Smoke was starting to hang around the fireplace, where it really shouldn't be.

She knew she'd opened the damper to the correct position, so she had no idea what might have happened.

She went outside to see if she could see any smoke coming out of the chimney, and she didn't see anything.

When she went back inside, the smoke was starting to waft around the living room.

She ran to open the windows and the sliding glass door that led to the deck so the smoke would have somewhere to go.

It wasn't a big deal. Sometimes fireplaces smoked a little. She'd just let the fire die down, and it would be fine.

But the fire was burning hotter than ever, and the smoke kept getting worse.

She coughed as she stood frozen for far too long, trying to figure out what to do.

She felt helpless, paralyzed, like the fire would simply overwhelm her.

Then she realized she was being stupid. She didn't need to wait for the fire to die down naturally. There must be a fire extinguisher somewhere in the house. She checked the closet where they kept household tools. She checked the kitchen—under the sink, in the pantry, then in every cabinet. She ran upstairs and checked the bedrooms, but she couldn't find one.

The smoke was getting worse. She started to panic.

What if, in her stupidity, she actually burned the house down?

It was a ridiculous thought. A fire safely in the fireplace was not going to burn the house down, no matter how much smoke it produced. Thus relieved by logic, she ran for her phone as she kept looking around for the fire extinguisher.

Daniel answered on the fourth ring. "What's wrong?" he asked by way of greeting. He would know she wouldn't bother him during a class unless there was an emergency, and there was concern in his tone.

"Nothing," she said. "I mean, it's not an emergency. It's just... Sorry, I shouldn't have interrupted you."

"Jessica, tell me what's going on." His voice snapped, but it was obviously from urgency.

"Don't we have a fire extinguisher somewhere?" she asked. Then she had the brainstorm to check the garage and found one on a shelf just outside the door. "Never mind," she said, wishing she hadn't called him. "Sorry to bother you."

"Wait, what's going—"

She'd already hung up the phone now and ran into the living room to put out the fire.

It extinguished quickly—if messily—and Jessica breathed a sigh of relief when the blaze died. The room was still smoky, but at least new smoke wasn't billowing in anymore.

She heard the sound of the front door open, but she didn't have time to process what it meant before Daniel's voice boomed out. "Are you okay? What's going on?"

"Nothing." She gasped, whirling around in surprise. "What are you doing here?"

He scanned the room, taking in the smoke and the fireplace. "You called to ask about a fire extinguisher. What did you expect me to do?"

"You didn't have to come back." She was mortified that she'd pulled him away from his church responsibilities for something so absurd. There had never been a more incompetent wife in the history of the world. "I had it under control."

He rubbed his eyes with the back of his hand, obviously rubbing away smoke. He still looked like he was in crisis mode, his shoulders tense and his posture poised. "I didn't know that."

"Sorry to scare you. The fireplace is broken or something. I don't know what happened."

He finally relaxed as he evidently processed the situation. "Well," he said, smiling at her fondly, adorably, "there's this little thing called a damper. And when you light a fire, you want to make sure—"

"I had it opened! I'm not completely stupid. Go look and see."

He walked over to check, coughing a few times at the lingering smoke, and then raised his eyebrows. "It is opened. Something must be broken."

He stuck his head practically into the fireplace to look up the chimney, and she made a startled exclamation and dragged him back. "Watch it. It's still hot in there."

"It must be broken."

"We can get it fixed this week. You can go back to church. Sorry to pull you away." Her fingers curled around his arm, and she loved how strong and solid he felt beneath her hands.

"It's fine. They just took a few minutes' break. It's freezing in here."

"I had to open the windows for the smoke." She coughed again and wiped the tears from the smoke off her face.

Daniel frowned at her in concern. "Well, go put another sweatshirt on. You'll be too cold in here."

"I'll be fine. You can go back."

"I don't want to leave you here in a freezing, smoky house."

"I'm fine. I'll keep blowing it out. The fire is out now, so it will go away soon. There's no emergency."

"The fire extinguisher should have been in a better place. I'll get a couple more of them tomorrow."

"Okay. You can do that tomorrow. But Daniel, all those prospective new members took time out of their Thursday evenings to attend this class, so you need to go back to them now."

"Yeah. Right." He was still eyeing in concern the room, slightly less smoky now.

"What did you tell them when you left, anyway?"

"Nothing."

He looked slightly sheepish.

"You told them you had to go keep me from burning the house down, didn't you?"

She could see from his expression that he'd said something very close to that.

She smiled ruefully. "It's fine. This time it wasn't my fault."

"That's right. Just an unfortunate accident." His mouth tightened in a familiar way.

"You can laugh if you want."

"I don't want to laugh."

"Yes, you do." She pushed him toward the door into the garage. "Now go back. Hopefully it will be less smoky when you get home."

She spent another hour trying to clear the room of smoke. Eventually the smoke was gone, although the smell lingered.

There was no cozy evening when Daniel got back. He'd stopped on his way home to buy four fire extinguishers, and he spent the rest of the evening trying to figure out what was wrong with the damper.

Jessica eventually gave up and went to take a long shower, trying to wash the smoke out of her hair.

She was exhausted and freezing and her throat hurt as she crawled into bed. She'd dried her hair as much as she had energy for, but it was still slightly damp.

She read until Daniel came up and took a shower too.

When he got into bed, he turned his head toward her. "Are you okay?"

"Fine. Does my hair still smell like smoke?"

He leaned over and smelled. "No."

"Liar. I keep smelling smoke."

"It's your imagination."

She grumbled and turned the light off.

A few minutes later, she heard repressed chuckling from his side of the bed. "What are you laughing at?" she demanded.

"Nothing."

"Is it my pitiful attempt at a roast or my almost burning down the house?"

"A little of both."

She couldn't help but chuckle too. "It hasn't been a very good week for me, I guess."

He rolled over until he was almost on top of her. His voice took on a particular resonance she was starting to recognize—one she only heard in the bedroom when the lights were off. "I think it's been a very exciting week."

"Well, I'm here for your amusement."

"Glad to hear it."

He was still laughing when he kissed her.

A few minutes later, when they'd both gotten excited and urgent, he asked in baffled frustration, "How many sweatshirts do you have on?"

# SEVEN

The following evening after dinner, Daniel went into his study to work.

After straightening up the kitchen, Jessica walked down the hall and stared at his closed door.

There wasn't anything wrong with his getting some work done in the evening. He didn't owe her anything except respect and faithfulness. She shouldn't expect for their practical marriage to turn into something romantic—just because she was wanting it more and more.

It felt wrong though. Like he was hiding from her. Like he was hiding from life. Like this was his way of clinging to certain things he couldn't yet let go of.

Glancing down at Bear, who was wagging her tail eagerly with her nose to the crack of the door, wanting to get at the person inside the room, Jessica felt a sudden swell of frustrated impatience.

She wanted to shake Daniel. To tell him to just get over it, to get it together. Life went on, and nothing worthwhile could be gained by wallowing in grief or wishing for something that could never happen—like his dead wife coming back to him.

She wasn't a fool though. That simply wasn't how people worked. It wasn't how grief worked.

No one could just shake themselves out of it.

"No, I think it's a good idea," Daniel said from inside the study. His voice was muffled but audible. He must be on the phone. "I think we can definitely plan something like that."

There was a pause, during which the other person must have spoken. Then Daniel continued, "Good. Just make sure you include other women in the church in planning it. Actually, you might ask Jessica. She'd be great at it."

Jessica was surprised since she couldn't think of any sort of church event that she would be great at planning. Maybe he was just continuing his mission to get her more involved and to act more like a typical pastor's wife.

"No," Daniel said. "You can't assume things like that. She could really help. She's brilliant. Seriously—she's one of the smartest people I know, and I'm not just saying that because I'm married to her. She's quiet, and she never puts herself out there, but that doesn't mean she can't contribute. Not everyone is comfortable jumping into new situations, so you need to make an extra effort to include them. Ask her. I guarantee she'll really be able help."

Jessica realized she was standing the hallway, shamelessly eavesdropping on a conversation that wasn't intended for her. She quickly walked back to the kitchen, feeling strange and confused.

She wasn't sure if she was touched that Daniel was making such a point of her being smart and capable, or if she was uncomfortable that he was throwing her into the game when she much preferred watching from the sidelines.

"Looks like it's just us this evening," Jessica said to Bear, trying to distract herself from the strange feeling. "What should we do?" She felt kind of lonely and heavy, like she wanted to mope.

It was stupid, but she'd never imagined she would be lonely after she got married.

Bear had flopped down on the floor as soon as they'd entered the kitchen, but now she sat up at Jessica's voice and begged.

"Food, huh?" Jessica glanced into the living room at the lit Christmas tree. It was only seven on a Friday evening, and Christmas was coming soon.

She might as well do something fun and productive, whether Daniel wanted to do it with her or not. She checked the cabinets, pulling out ingredients for the one thing she really knew how to make well.

Every year about this time, her mother would make caramel corn and fill decorated jars with it to give as Christmas presents.

She didn't have enough ingredients to make it for presents, but she could at least make one batch to eat.

It had always been one of her favorite times growing up, making caramel corn with her mother. She turned on some Christmas music and sang with the songs as she worked.

She was feeling better when the batch was done, and she even braved the fireplace again.

The damper had been fixed yesterday, so this time the blaze ignited to create a cozy ambience instead of a smoky room.

She'd poured herself a glass of wine and put some of the finished popcorn in a bowl to carry into the living room when she glanced back down the hall.

She didn't have to shake him out of his brooding. She could just invite him to come out. If he rejected her, then he rejected her. It wasn't the end of the world.

And she was somehow sure that hiding in his study wasn't good for him right now.

She tapped on his door and opened it when he answered.

He was sitting at his desk but not working on the computer. It looked like he was just reading. He'd obviously finished the phone call.

"You can read out in the living room, you know," she said, making a point of not glancing over to the photo of Lila that was sitting on his desk.

He raised his eyebrows.

"You don't have to, but you can if you want. I won't disturb you. I made a fire, and it's really nice in there. Plus there's caramel corn."

She kept her voice light as she smiled at him. "Just come on out if you want any."

She was pleased with the attempt as she left the study, but then she glanced down at herself. She wore a gray sweatshirt with red and black plaid flannel pants.

She really should have worn something more flattering if she'd wanted to lure her husband out of his study. She was absolutely terrible at being attractive. Most of the time, she didn't even remember to check the mirror.

Nothing to do about it now though. He'd already seen her in her baggy clothes.

She'd settled on the couch with her laptop on her lap and the bowl of caramel corn on the couch cushion beside her when Daniel appeared.

She smiled at him in surprise.

"You said there was caramel corn," he said by way of explanation.

She couldn't help but laugh. "There is."

He sat down beside her and grabbed a handful. "Just like your mom's," he said when he'd mostly chewed his first bite.

She was ridiculously pleased by the sentiment.

"Do I get any wine?" he asked, when she raised her glass to take a sip.

"You do if you haul yourself up to pour a glass."

She was just teasing and didn't mind getting him a glass, but he beat her to it, heaving himself back to his feet with a chuckle.

He returned to sit on the same spot, with just the bowl of caramel corn between them.

Jessica did her best not to feel ridiculously giddy. It shouldn't have been a big deal, but getting him out of his study tonight felt like a victory.

"What are you reading?" she asked, when he picked up his book. "Don't tell me Bonhoeffer."

"It's just some background reading on Acts."

She knew his next sermon series would be on the book of Acts. "You should read something just for fun."

"Bonhoeffer is for fun."

Rolling her eyes, she muttered, "You're just weird."

He seemed to be hiding a smile. "And what are *you* doing that's so normal?"

She glanced at the screen of her laptop. "Just going over some work. Nothing too intense."

"You shouldn't be working so late."

She snorted at the appalling irony of that statement, but she answered, "I spent the afternoon with Mom, so I actually have time I need to make up."

"I thought you could work some at your mom's."

"Sometimes I can, but she was pretty lucid today. She kept wanting to talk."

He smiled for real, obviously sensing how pleased she was by this fact. "What did she talk about?"

"Old times. She likes to rehearse. She told me the story of your breaking her window with the baseball about four times."

He gave an exaggerated groan. "I'm never going to live that down." He paused for a moment before he added, "I used to love when she made caramel corn."

"I know you did. You always somehow knew and 'accidentally' stopped by."

"I could always hear you singing."

"What?"

"You and your mom would always be singing Christmas songs as you made it."

"Oh. Yeah. I guess we did."

"I heard you singing earlier, and I knew you were making caramel corn."

"Well, why didn't you accidentally happen by the kitchen?"

"I was considering it."

His voice was light, but she studied his face, and she suddenly knew he *had* considered it but then decided against it.

If she hadn't gone to get him, he wouldn't have come out at all.

She was really glad she had.

Inspired by this, she took another risk. "Do you want to come Christmas shopping with me tomorrow?"

"What?"

"You're taking tomorrow off, right? You said you weren't planning to go on the hike with the youth group." He got one weekday off every week since he always had to work on Sundays, and he was supposed to have Saturdays off too, although he usually ended up doing prep for Sunday or some other church event.

"Yeah, I don't need to go on that hike."

"I was thinking about going Christmas shopping. I need to buy some presents since it's coming up soon and I have nothing. I was just asking if you wanted to come with me if you weren't going on the hike."

He gave her a surprised quirk of his lips. "Yeah. I'll go with you. I've got to get some presents too."

"Just make sure you get something really good for me."

"I was thinking about maybe some cooking lessons."

She gasped in outrage, but his teasing expression was impossible to take seriously. "Fine. Then I'm going to get you some auto-repair classes."

"I'm great at cars!"

"Right."

"I really am."

"You're still not touching mine."

They fell into a comfortable silence, both of them munching on caramel corn and staring at the fire.

"What are you thinking about?" he asked her at last.

She blushed since she'd actually been thinking about how amazing and adorable he was. Since she couldn't possibly admit she'd been thinking fond thoughts about him, she said instead, "Thinking about Christmas. I used to love your family's Christmas parties."

"I didn't."

"Why not? They were always so beautiful. The house was gorgeously decorated, and everyone would dress up, and the food was delicious, and everyone would gather around the piano and sing carols." She sighed at the memory. "It felt like something out of an old movie. I just loved those parties."

"You should have seen the flurry that went into preparations. My mom would stress about those parties for weeks beforehand. And I hated to dress up. I hated having to help clean the house and serve the food."

"Well, that's too bad. Those parties were really special. I looked forward to them from the time we got the invitation. It was just me and my mom most of the time, but at those parties it always felt like I was part of a..."

"A what?" His voice had changed.

She shrugged and glanced away from him. "I don't know. Part of a community. A family. Like there were a lot of people who were all connected to me deeply."

He was silent for a moment after she'd said it, as if he were letting the words soak in. Then, "And yet you always try to hide now."

"I do not try to hide!" Even as she vehemently disagreed, she wasn't entirely convinced he was wrong. "Why do you always go on about that? I do like being alone sometimes, but I want to feel connected. And... I don't. Most of the time I just... I just don't anymore."

Her voice cracked on the last word, and she felt like an absolute idiot. It had been a casual conversation, and she'd just blurted out something really private.

"You are," he said softly, responding to the newly serious mood. He reached out and put a hand on her thigh.

"I don't really know that I am." She couldn't look at him, so she stared at the crackling fire. Her face blazed with the heat wafting from the flames.

"You're still part of this town, Jessica."

"I guess. I just don't really feel like part of it. It's not the same." One of the reasons she'd wanted this marriage was so that she could feel connected again, and it was so frustrating that even marriage hadn't made her less lonely. Hadn't made her less alone.

"It *is* the same. These people know you and love you. You're the one who holds herself back."

"I do not hold myself back." Her voice was a little sharp since it felt like he was turning on her when he'd sounded so understanding before. "Name one time I was invited to do something social and refused."

"That's not what I mean. I mean holding yourself back emotionally, like you don't think they'll love you."

"Believe it or not, people don't always love me." For some reason, the pragmatic words sounded almost poignant to her own ears.

"They do. They would—if you would just take a step out and let them. But you assume they're all judging you or looking down on you or ignoring you or something."

"Not all of them." This was far deeper a conversation than she had expected this evening, and it left her feeling a little off stride. But she was on the defensive now, and she was determined to stand up for herself. "But you can't tell me some of these Willow Park women don't think I'm unnatural for spending time on a career instead of taking care of a house."

"Some of them might. They're not perfect. But who is? Narrow views can be incredibly annoying, but these people only know what they've been around all their lives. They'll never realize they're wrong unless they get to know you, and they'll never get to know you if you don't let them."

Daniel was good at this—seeing people clearly, giving advice, thinking of what other people needed and putting together a convincing case for it. He did it naturally, and it was part of his job.

But for some reason, it felt like he was invading her soul, and she wasn't entirely comfortable with what it revealed about her.

"Being connected to other people doesn't happen magically, you know," he added, a dry smile in his voice. "You've got to do some of it yourself. You have to take a risk. You have to let yourself be vulnerable."

"Fine, fine. I'll try to be better. Shall we have a little self-help session with you now?"

He chuckled. "I'd rather not."

"That's what I thought. You can dish it out but can't take it. Typical."

He stood up, smiling at her grumpy face. "Do you want some more wine?"

"Yeah." She handed him her glass and stared at the fire until he returned.

"The tree looks great," he said sitting down again and grabbing another handful of caramel corn. "Except it's missing something."

"What?" She scanned the tree, which she thought looked perfect.

"Why didn't any of my peanuts end up on the tree?"

She choked as she remembered the peanuts painted in red and green he'd made in elementary school. She'd seen them in his ornament box but had passed them over.

"I don't know," she murmured smoothly. "I must have missed them."

"They're my favorites. I made them when I was seven."

"They look like it."

"Ah ha! I knew you rejected them on purpose!"

"I must have missed them when I was decorating the tree, but I remembered them when you mentioned them just now."

"Don't try to con me. You did it on purpose. I'll find them tomorrow and add them to the tree."

"I think it looks good now."

"It will look better with the peanuts."

"It will look ridiculous with the peanuts."

"They'll give it character."

"Yeah, character like a nursery school."

"What's wrong with that?"

"Nothing, if the tree is *in* a nursery school. Our tree has plenty of character without them."

"Lila always let me put them on."

"Well, I'm not Lila."

The argument had been fun and playful, but suddenly the mood shifted.

Wishing she hadn't said the final comment, Jessica stared at the fire for a minute. "Sorry," she said at last.

"Don't be."

She glanced at him and saw he didn't look upset. Poignant but not upset.

It gave her courage enough to pursue the topic. She wanted him to be able to talk about Lila with her. She didn't want Lila to be this silent, impenetrable barrier between them. "Did you and Lila have any traditions for Christmas?"

He shrugged, and she didn't think he was going to answer. But then, staring at the fire the way she'd done before, he murmured, "Not many. We always had breakfast in bed on Christmas morning. Then we'd exchanged gifts right there."

"In bed? You didn't even do it in front of the tree?"

"No. Our first Christmas, she was so excited that she couldn't wait until we'd gotten out of bed. So she pulled the present out of the nightstand and thrust it at me."

"What had she gotten you?"

"A pen. A really nice one. One I'd always wanted."

"Oh. That sounds like a great gift."

Her chest hurt. Lila and Daniel had loved each other so much. She remembered when they first started dating when he was a senior in college and Lila was a sophomore. Jessica well recalled that familiar sense of certainty—the absolute knowledge, from the very beginning, that they would be together forever.

She'd known it for sure. She'd seen their whole future spilling out before then. He and Lila would fall in love, marry, have children, spend their lives together. Love each other until they died.

That future was cut short, and she had a sudden slice of guilt about feeling a little grateful about it since it meant she could have at least a little part of him now.

Nothing about Lila's death was good, but if she hadn't died, Jessica would never have known, loved, married Daniel.

The thoughts were too hard, too deep, for a winter evening in front of the fire. She shook them off for another time.

To distract herself, she tossed a piece of caramel corn to Bear, who'd been sitting with perfect posture in the hope that her good behavior would prompt an edible reward.

Bear caught the kernel neatly in her mouth.

"You shouldn't give that dog people food." Daniel must have, like her, broken away from the poignancy of the moment before.

"A little caramel corn never hurt anyone."

"It's the principle."

She was tempted to tell him she'd seen him give Bear a piece of roast, but she managed to refrain—since he'd clearly done so in secret. She tossed another piece which was also caught. "She's very talented."

"You're making it easy on her by throwing it right at her mouth."

She frowned and tossed another piece, slightly misdirected.

Bear reached for it smartly and caught it.

Jessica gave Daniel a triumphant look.

"I'm not sure that was anything to be proud of." He tossed a piece, not anywhere close to the dog.

Bear jumped up and lunged, grabbing it just after it hit the floor.

"She couldn't possibly have caught that one! You have to make it achievable!"

"Fine." He tossed again, this one just slightly closer.

Bear hurried to snatch up the popcorn and didn't care at all that she hadn't caught it.

"You're making her miss on purpose."

He was about to toss another piece—this one no doubt far afield too—but Jessica reached over and grabbed his wrist before he did.

They had a little wrestling match over the piece of popcorn, broken only by Daniel saving the bowl of popcorn before it spilled and Jessica moving her laptop to the coffee table before it fell to the floor.

He'd clenched his hand over the piece, but she used both of hers to try to pry his fingers open. They were both laughing now, and she was draped on top of them, but she wasn't about to give up.

He was stronger than her though, and she couldn't make his fingers budge.

She groaned in frustration and made like she was going to give up.

When he relaxed slightly, she tickled him under the arm.

He huffed in surprise, and his fist loosened.

She clawed the popcorn out of his palm, in the process disintegrating it completely.

"I got it!" she declared, holding up a tiny piece as a victory prize. "I win! I—"

Her gloating was broken off abruptly when he grabbed her and pushed her back onto the couch, using his weight to hold her in place. "You did not fight fair."

"It was perfectly fair. You're just a sore loser." Her voice wasn't as authoritative as she'd been trying for. In fact, it was a little shaky.

She was suddenly conscious of his strength and heat and hot brown eyes as he gazed down on her. His skin was slightly damp, and his lower body was pressing into hers.

Her heart hammered wildly when he lowered his face to kiss her.

His mouth was gentle at first, almost sweet, his tongue gently teasing her lips. Then he nudged inside her mouth and started to stroke, and she moaned deep in her throat as her body responded.

Her blood pulsed as she fisted her hands in his shirt, meeting his tongue with her own.

They'd never kissed like this before outside the bedroom. Before, it had always been in the dark.

The difference didn't matter though. She responded as she always did, desperately eager for more.

She arched her neck and gasped loudly as his mouth lowered to that spot on her neck that felt so good. "Daniel."

He grunted a response, his hands starting to move busily over her body. They slipped under her sweatshirt and tank until they touched her bare skin.

She shivered as he pushed the fabric up to bare her breasts. Then she pressed up into his hands, making a silly breathless squeak as he thumbed her nipples.

He'd been staring hungrily down at her body but now he glanced up at her face. "What was that sound?"

"What sound?"

"That squeak."

"I didn't hear a squeak."

He thumbed her nipples again, and she made the same little squeak at the resulting jolt of pleasure.

He grinned down at her, obviously very pleased with himself. "*That* sound."

"It wasn't a squeak. I was just breathing."

"I know a squeak when I hear one." He used the pads of his thumbs to rub circles on her tightened nipples, and she bit her lip to hold back the sound this time.

But he kept it up, and it felt so good, and she couldn't help but arch up and release a ragged sigh.

"Beautiful," he murmured. "I love that you're so responsive."

She adored the possessive sound of his voice, but she couldn't respond with words until he released her breasts and slid his hands down to her hips.

"What's to love about that?" she asked, glad to hear at least a tiny bit of irony in her tone.

He grabbed the waistband of her pants. "It makes me feel all manly."

"It's not about you, so don't get a big head about it."

He raised his eyebrows sky-high.

She gasped. "You know what I meant!"

He laughed as he leaned down to kiss her again. "Yes, I know what you meant."

He evidently changed his mind about her waistband and instead moved his hands back up to her breasts as he kissed her. He fondled her until she was squirming and had wrapped one leg around his hip, trying to get friction where she needed it.

Their mouths parted long enough for him to pull her tops over her head, but then he kissed her again. The fire against her bare skin burned, blazed, branded her.

His lips trailed down her neck again, this time descending to her collarbone. "So beautiful," he murmured. "You're so beautiful, Jessica. I can't seem to get enough of you."

Her heart swelled in pleasure at the words. Then at the sensations as his mouth moved over her breasts, teasing for a minute before they lowered to her belly.

She cried out when he reached up to caress her breasts as he kissed little lines over her abdomen.

The ache between her legs intensified until she couldn't stand it. "Please, Daniel. Please. I need… I need…"

She writhed beneath his attentions.

He knew what she needed, however inarticulate she was. He pulled down her pants and panties together and dropped them over the side of the couch.

Then he stared down at her completely naked body.

She'd never bared herself like this to anyone in a completely lit room. He could see all of her, and his eyes raked over her body, settling over the juncture of her thighs.

Then his eyes blazed, and his head lowered, and his mouth nuzzled her intimately.

She clutched at his head as he explored with his tongue and lips, fisting her hands in his hair.

When he found her clit, he sucked on it until she was crying out loudly and her whole body shook through an intense orgasm.

"Oh, wow, oh, wow, oh, wow," she mumbled when he finally raised his head.

He smiled, clearly proud of himself as he wiped his mouth with the back of his hand.

She gazed up at him. He looked so strong and sweet and dryly amused and everything she'd ever wanted.

She grabbed him and pulled him down into a kiss.

He responded eagerly, just as passionate as her. He worked on his pants and she worked on his shirt until he was naked too.

She couldn't help but reach out for his erection, stroking it gently with her fingers.

His breath hitched and then hitched again as she caressed him.

She wondered if he'd felt the same pleased pride she did when he'd pleased her.

He let her explore for a minute or so, but then he moved her hands away and eased her onto her back on the couch.

She reached up to grab the armrest above her head and hold on as he slid himself inside her.

His thrusts were fast and steady, and they felt increasingly good—tight and full and intimate.

She panted as he rocked into her, and she fisted her fingers into the leather, her whole body shaking with his motion.

He paused to wrap her legs around his hips, and she locked her ankles and tightened her thighs on each of his thrusts.

"Oh, yeah, oh, yeah." She gasped when the penetration shifted inside her. "So good."

She'd never felt like this before, like pressure inside her was coiling, even deeper than her orgasms before.

"How is it?" He was sweating and huffing with effort, but pleasure twisted on his face.

When she could focus enough to look in his eyes, she saw their expression was strangely primal, dominant.

"So good. Don't stop. Please don't stop." She was practically begging now as the pleasure kept spiraling through her. She was slammed with waves of heat from the fire and so much more.

"I won't stop. That's right, Jessica. That's right. That's so good. You're almost there."

His voice was another caress. She started to make embarrassing sobbing noises, and her hands flew up to claw at his shoulders as the tension finally broke.

Her release was too loud. Her whole body seemed to come undone. Then she heard him make a loud, extended guttural sound as he jerked a few last times into her clenching body.

His climax was obviously just as powerful as hers. He collapsed on top of her.

Her throat hurt. And it was so hot. And so incredibly good.

"That was... That was..." She couldn't begin to complete the sentence.

"Yeah."

She hugged him, unable to not convey the wash of affection and connection she was flooded with. He hugged her back.

After a minute, she said, "I can't believe we did it on the couch."

"At least it wasn't on the floor. That can lead to uncomfortable side effects."

"Rug burn?"

"Or bruises."

She laughed, and he was chuckling too as he pressed a few clumsy kisses against her mouth.

Her heart felt like it exploded in her chest, as powerful as her body had exploded.

She knew he needed this. Knew she was giving to him. Knew she had something important to offer him, and it wasn't only physical.

She knew it—the way she'd never known it before.

"I don't know if I can move," he groaned, still resting his weight on her.

"You're going to have to soon. You're kind of heavy."

He groaned again but managed to pull off her.

They found their clothes and then kind of sat there, as if neither was sure what to do.

"You look worn out," she said, looking at his damp face and tired eyes.

"I am."

"Well, then let's go to bed."

It was as good a thing to do as anything else.

They went upstairs, and after they got ready and climbed into bed, he took her in his arms.

She was feeling blissfully content and sleepy when she was suddenly jarred by an impact on the mattress.

She knew what it was immediately. Bear had jumped on the bed. Daniel grunted and lifted his head.

"Get down," she said, too drowsy and replete to sound very firm. "Bear, get down."

Bear ignored her and started to scratch up a nest at the bottom of the bed between Daniel's legs and Jessica's where there really wasn't much room.

"Down." Daniel's voice carried much more authority than hers had, but the dog showed no reaction as she settled into a ball to sleep.

Worried that Daniel would be annoyed, Jessica nudged the dog with her foot, trying to give her a push off the bed. All it accomplished was Bear heaving a huge sigh and stretching out at her full length across the bottom of the bed.

With a groan, Jessica sat up and tried to push the dog with her hands.

Bear lifted her head to aim a look of victimized indignation at her owner before heaving herself to her feet and jumping off the bed.

Relieved, Jessica cuddled up beside Daniel again.

Two minutes later, the mattress shifted dramatically again.

"What is her problem tonight?" Daniel asked.

"Sometimes she just wants on the bed. I can never figure out why. She's been really good lately."

"This is what you call good?"

"Don't be grumpy with her. I'll try to get her off."

Jessica tried pushing with her feet again. And then with her hands. The dog huffed and moved to the far side of the bed, where Jessica normally slept when she wasn't pressed up against Daniel. Evidently assuming she'd be safe there, Bear gave Jessica's pillow a few scratches and then flopped down to sleep.

"She sleeps on your pillow?" Daniel's voice was astounded.

"She normally sleeps at the bottom, but she thought she wasn't supposed to because I kept pushing her."

"She isn't supposed to sleep at the bottom. She isn't supposed to sleep on the bed at all."

"She's all the way on my side and not touching you at all. If you want her off, then you need to get up, walk around the bed, and pick her up to put her back on the floor."

"It seems pretty clear that would be wasted energy since she'd just jumped back up again."

"All I'm saying is that, if you want her down, you need to put her down yourself."

"I can put her in one of the spare rooms and shut the door."

"I guarantee that would not end up well for you."

He released a long, resigned breath and adjusted his arm around her, pulling her more comfortably against his side. "Dogs don't belong on the bed."

"She sleeps on her own bed most of the time."

"She should sleep on her bed all the time."

He didn't really sound annoyed, so Jessica smiled. "She's not hurting anything. She's not anywhere close to you."

"It's the principle."

"She doesn't understand principles. Moral training just doesn't work on a dog."

He chuckled. "As long as she doesn't try to take my pillow."

She pressed a kiss against his chest. "She'll have to get past me to get to your pillow."

"Good. You can be my barrier against any encroaching dogs."

"That's what I'm here for."

"I knew I was keeping you around for some reason."

His voice was low and fond. His body was warm and solid. His arm was strong and deliciously possessive. And his heart was the kindest she'd ever known.

She felt safe. Felt needed. Felt cared for. It wasn't long before she drifted into sleep.

Just before she did, she decided she didn't need anything more than this.

# EIGHT

Jessica woke up and felt chilled, so she rolled over instinctively toward Daniel's side of the bed.

She kept rolling until she almost rolled off.

Bear had gotten down sometime during the night. It was still dark in the room, and staring at the clock for several seconds finally produced the knowledge that it was two thirty in the morning.

Daniel wasn't in bed.

Jessica sat up, blinking and listening. He could just be in the bathroom.

He wasn't though. The light was off, and the door was hanging opened.

She knew where he was.

She got up, slid on her slippers, and pulled on a sweatshirt since it was cool in the house.

She walked slowly downstairs and through the hall to the study.

The door was half-opened, so she stood in the dark hallway and looked inside.

The only light was the desk lamp, and it illuminated the room with a dim glow, casting weird shadows on the floor and walls. Daniel sat in his normal spot at the desk. His Bible was opened in front of him, and he held his head up with both hands as he read.

He was hunched, heavy, wounded somehow. She could see it in his posture, in the way his fingers closed around his hair.

Her heart went out to him with such power that her eyes burned. She'd thought he'd had a good evening with her, but he was hurting so much. Still so much.

And he simply refused to let her help.

She watched for a long time, standing silently in the hall, praying for him, praying for both of them.

She didn't think she'd made a noise, but eventually he jerked his head up quickly, as if he'd somehow realized she was there.

His eyes were blank, almost dazed, like he couldn't figure out what she was doing there.

"Are you all right?" she asked, her voice cracking oddly.

She'd felt so close to him this evening. She'd felt loved, even though he'd never said it. But evidently the evening hadn't meant what she'd thought it meant. If anything, it had made him feel worse.

He opened his mouth to answer, but no words came out. Then he glanced to the side and let out a breath. Finally he hoarsely spoke what was obviously the naked truth. "I... I don't know."

"You can tell me, you know. You can tell me anything."

He still looked dazed as he turned his head to stare at her again. The picture of Lila wasn't set out on the desk for some reason. She didn't know what to make of that. She always assumed he came in here at night to brood about missing her.

"Are you still feeling guilty?" she asked at last.

He shook his head.

She didn't think he would open up to her about something so deep out of the blue like this under normal circumstances, but he'd be down here wrestling spiritually for who knew how long, and he had no defenses left. "Not guilty."

"Then what is it? It looks like something is eating you alive."

"I'm..."

When he trailed off, glancing away again, she stepped into the study. "You're what?"

"I'm still so angry."

She sucked in a breath, shocked by the words, by the sentiment.

Daniel had always been the most mature, devout man she'd ever known. He'd always seemed to have such a clear sense of God's will. While she'd floundered spiritually more than once in her life, he never seemed to have done so.

She never would have dreamed of him feeling something like this.

"I know it's wrong. I know I have no right to be angry. But I can't get over it. I can't reconcile. I'm just so angry." He clenched the hand that was resting just next to his Bible, which was opened to Job, she noticed. "I just can't let it go."

A tear streamed down her cheek, although she hadn't realized she was close to tears. She wiped it away impatiently. "I think anger is normal. It's a part of grief. Right?"

"This is more than a stage of grief. I went through all the regular stages. I'm nothing but angry now. It just feels so wrong that he takes away everything from me, everything I want. It infects everything. I can't let myself want anything else because he'll just... The whole world just feels..."

She was holding her breath, but she finally had to let it go when he didn't finish. "Feels what?"

"Broken."

The word hung in the air—rough and soft and achingly honest.

Heartbreaking.

She opened her mouth to reply but closed it again, afraid to say what she wanted, afraid it would come across as preachy or judgmental, which would only make things worse.

He must have seen her hesitation because he murmured, "You can say it."

Since he asked for it, she did. "I thought you always said that the world feels broken because it *is* broken. And that we lie to ourselves when we assume it should somehow be different for us. I thought you said faith doesn't sugarcoat reality. It shows the truth for what it is. Sometimes it's incredibly hard, but it isn't always... dark."

Daniel had said all that. From the pulpit and out of it. She'd heard versions of the same truth over and over again. She'd always believed it as much as he had, and she thought it was what he needed to hear right now.

It didn't appear to make an impact though. He gazed at her for a long time, and she thought she saw again that kind of deep yearning, as if he desperately wanted something, desperately wanted *her*.

She stared back, wanting him just as much, loving him more than she'd realized was possible, feeling the same kind of longing she saw in him.

But she didn't know how to reach him. "Maybe…" Her voice broke so painfully she had to clear her throat.

He just watched her, waiting for her to finish.

"Maybe you're not letting him give you anything good."

It was a several seconds before he answered. As he did, he broke their shared gaze. "Maybe. You might be right. But even that feels broken to me, because he gives and takes away. I can't seem to get past that. Sometimes I'll forget it, for a little while, for just a minute, but then I'll remember again, and it all comes crashing down, even more broken than before."

She understood. That was her. Helping him forget for a little while. But only for a little while.

She didn't make it better for him after all. She never would.

It hurt. So much. She took a shaky breath and forced down the response since this was about him, not about her. "What can I do?"

"Nothing." The words were final.

But he was a tenderhearted man—tender to the core of his being—and he glanced back up to her face and said rather raspingly, "But thank you."

∼

She woke up the next morning to someone shaking her shoulder.

She thought she was awake, but she couldn't pry her eyes open. She tried to pull away from the hand, but it was too strong.

Then came a grating voice. "I'm sorry, Jessica. Can you wake up for a minute? Then you can go back to sleep."

She didn't want to wake up. It felt like she'd only just fallen asleep.

She mumbled and tried to roll over onto her other side.

The hand turned her back over. "Jessica," came the voice again. "I don't want to leave without explaining."

With great effort, she managed to get her eyes halfway opened. Daniel knelt next to the bed, fully dressed in a flannel shirt over a thermal T-shirt.

That seemed strange, but she didn't know why. If only her mind was working better.

"Hi," she croaked. She had no idea what was happening, but it was nice to see Daniel so close to her, his brown eyes focused on her face.

She smiled, and she thought his face changed for a minute, but she couldn't quite identify the transformation.

Then his expression returned to what it had been, and he shook her shoulder again. "Are you awake?"

"What's going on?"

"I'm sorry to wake you up."

"S'okay."

"I didn't want to be gone when you woke up."

Now her mind was starting to work. No wonder things felt wrong. "Gone where?"

"I'm going on the hiking trip with the youth group."

"But you weren't going on that. You said you didn't have to. You were going Christmas shopping with me."

"I know. But I've been thinking about it, and I think it's best that I go. I don't want to look like a slacker when I've only just gotten this job."

She couldn't imagine anyone would think he was a slacker for not going on an all-day hiking trip with teenagers when he wasn't the leader of the youth group and had no obligation to go with them.

Then the evening before came flooding back to her. The laughter, the tenderness, the intimacy, the heartbreaking conversation in his study.

He wasn't going on the hike because he felt he should.

He was going to get some distance from her.

"We were going shopping," she said rather stupidly.

"I know. But you'll be more productive without me anyway. I'd just slow you down."

That was absurd. Her chest was starting to hurt so much she raised a hand to her breastbone. "I thought you were going with me."

She hated the sound of her voice. Pitiful. Needy.

"I really should go hiking instead."

"Oh." She wasn't going to beg, and she was absolutely not going to cry because he'd made a decision to pull away from her. "Okay."

His face looked torn for just a moment. Then he stood up. "I'll be back late."

"Oh. Okay."

"Have a good day."

The only thing she could say was what she'd already said twice, so she didn't say anything as he walked out of the room.

He wore jeans and hiking boots and looked rugged and outdoorsy.

He was strong and handsome and brilliant and tender. And broken.

She listened until she heard his old truck pull out of the driveway.

∼

She went shopping, just as she'd planned.

She fought the crowds and got all the presents on her list and all the wrapping supplies she needed.

When she got home, it wasn't even three yet, so she put on Christmas music and wrapped all her presents, singing as loud as she could to fool herself into being happy.

She didn't let herself think about Daniel. Instead, she watched TV as she ate dinner, and then she worked until almost ten, when her eyes started drooping.

Daniel wasn't home yet. He'd said he'd be late.

She went to take a shower and got into bed.

Bear walked up to the side of the bed and eyed her pitifully.

It was a big bed, and no one was in it but her. Bear obviously believed there was no reason she couldn't share.

"All right," Jessica said.

That was all the invitation Bear needed. She hurled herself up on the bed and tried to make a nest on Daniel's pillow, but Jessica managed to dissuade her from this unwise plan.

Instead, Jessica coaxed her into stretching out between the edge of the bed and Jessica's body so Daniel would have no reason to complain.

He might still complain, but she didn't care. If he was going to abandon her, then he couldn't whine about her taking comfort in her dog.

Jessica was exhausted but couldn't sleep. She lay in the dark and listened to Bear snore.

Surely the youth group wouldn't stay out this late, not when the next day was Sunday.

Maybe something happened.

Maybe someone had gotten hurt.

Maybe Daniel had gotten hurt.

She was just working herself up into a panic when she heard the truck in the driveway.

She let out a breath of relief.

She heard as he entered the house and walked up the stairs. Then she heard the door open and his footsteps come into the room.

She was facing the wall, toward Bear, and she didn't roll over. Didn't speak. Didn't move.

She didn't know what to say, so it was probably best that he thought she was asleep.

She didn't hear anything for a minute, but it felt like he was standing there, staring at her.

It made her feel weird. Vulnerable. And she was relieved when she heard him go into the bathroom.

The shower came on for a while. Then she heard the toilet flush and the water in the sink.

Then there was nothing left. He came back into the room and climbed into bed beside her.

She was closer to his side than normal because Bear was taking up a lot of room.

She still didn't turn toward him.

She was asleep.

"Are you angry?" he asked, his low voice startling in the dark room.

She jerked slightly but didn't turn to look at him. "Why would I be angry?"

"I don't know. It feels like you're angry."

And that annoyed her enough to make her turn over. "You don't know? You're telling me you don't know?"

"I'm sorry if you're disappointed about shopping, but that's a pretty minor thing to get worked up about."

"You know very well I'm not upset about that. Don't act like I'm being immature or irrational. This isn't about me."

She couldn't see his face well in the dark, but she could tell he was now just as annoyed as she was. "So it's about *me*? Tell me exactly what you think it's about."

"It's about you... I don't know... running away or something."

"From what?"

"From living your life."

"This is my life. This is my job. Going on the hike—"

"That's not what I'm talking about, and you know it. There's more to life that you're not letting in, and you're just... you're just running away from it because you think God takes away everything that's good."

"And what exactly do you think I should be letting into my life that I'm not?" His voice was icy cold now. "This marriage has never been romantic. We've never pretended it was. So to expect me to—"

"I'm not expecting you to do anything but be yourself, and you're not being that. I don't know why all these issues have caught up to you since we got married, but they have and they're changing you, and we both know it's not good for you. I can't even be your friend if you keep closing me out."

"I'm not closing you out. We spent all evening together yesterday. I can't spend every day with you."

She made a frustrated burst of sound that woke up Bear.

The dog gave a huff and jumped off the bed, pacing over to her bed and flopping down there instead.

Jessica scooted over to the warmth the dog had left behind, so she wasn't quite so close to Daniel.

"I'm not expecting you to spend every day with me. I'm expecting you to be yourself. To be real. And to live out what you believe. You're not doing any of that. You're just stewing. I understand you can't heal overnight, but I don't know if you're even really trying."

"Would you like to explain that?" His voice was clipped, like ice pellets. She'd never heard that tone from him before. Not directed to her, anyway.

"I don't even know what I mean. It just seems like you're stewing this way because it's safer than moving on, risking being hurt again. I don't know—"

She was rambling now, pouring out things she hadn't even acknowledged to herself. They felt right to her, but she never would have dared to say them had she not been so upset and frustrated.

Daniel broke into her rambles. "Your pop psychology is very impressive, but you clearly know nothing about me or about human nature at all—if you can trivialize something serious."

"I wasn't trivializing—"

"That's it. The conversation is over."

His voice was one she recognized. Absolute authority. It silenced her.

She wasn't going to keep reaching out to someone who didn't want her. She'd taken all the risks she was capable of taking with him. She retreated into herself—the only place it was genuinely safe—rolling over toward the wall and curling up in a pose of sleep.

She didn't sleep. She played out the argument in her mind, over and over again.

She stayed awake for hours, her back to Daniel, coming up with better responses and convincing him to see the light.

There was no light. Not until morning.

She must have fallen asleep at some point. When she became aware again, she rolled over.

Daniel's place was empty again.

When she got up to go downstairs to let out Bear and get some coffee, she saw he wasn't even in the house.

He'd left a note on the kitchen table.

"Gone to church early."

And that was fine.

That was perfectly fine.

She didn't want to talk to him either.

# NINE

Jessica took Bear for a long walk that morning and then got dressed for church, wearing a festive red sweater to try to cheer herself up.

It didn't work. She felt glum and exhausted and like she wanted to shake Daniel. She was ready to go fifteen minutes before she needed to leave for Sunday school, so she just sat on the window seat in the bedroom and stared out at the backyard. It was a gray day and blowing snow, and she watched little whirlwinds of snowflakes start up and subside against the frozen grass.

Christmas was just three days away.

As she stared, she noticed that the door to the workshop shed was hanging opened. Every once in a while a breeze would pick it up and blow it out farther and then bang it back.

She watched it for a minute or two, until she realized she should go close it so Daniel's tools wouldn't get damaged or stolen.

Willow Park was about as safe a town as one could get, but nowhere was free from crime, and Daniel had some expensive tools that might be a temptation.

She got up and walked downstairs and out to the yard. The wind was biting cold as she made her way across the yard to the shed, and it whipped her skirt around her legs. Even with tights and boots, she'd been stupid to wear a skirt this morning.

She grabbed the door as another gust blew it farther opened, and she was about to close it when she glanced inside.

Her eyes widened in surprise when she saw a large piece of wooden furniture. She pulled the cord to the light and closed the door against the wind as she stepped all the way inside.

It was a desk—made to fit in a corner, with three raised platforms. For monitors, she realized.

It was huge, made of gorgeous walnut, and really well put together. Daniel was obviously midway through polishing it.

It was for her. There was no other explanation. It was made to go in the corner near the windows of her office, just like he'd suggested that first day they were planning out the layout of the house.

She didn't think he'd ever made anything so ambitious before. She hadn't realized he was capable of making something like this. It must have taken him forever.

He'd done it for her. So many hours of work.

She gazed at the beautiful piece with slightly blurry eyes, unable to process what it meant, why he'd done it, how this fit with all the ways he'd been pulling away from her.

She ran her fingers over the smooth surface, her throat painfully tight.

She didn't understand. She didn't understand any of this.

The door to this workshop hadn't been opened yesterday evening. She would have noticed it. Which meant he'd come out here in the middle of the night to work on the desk some more.

She looked at his tools, neatly lined up on the work table and hanging on hooks. She tried to imagine what he was thinking all the time he was out here working on the desk. Then she noticed a glimpse of color and walked closer to see what it was.

A photo, a little bent and ragged around the edges, held down by a hammer.

She realized it was probably a picture of Lila—like the one he kept on his desk in the study, a memory of the life he'd really wanted and not the life he had.

Feeling the need to remind herself of this brutal truth, she stepped close enough to see the photo.

She frowned in surprise when she made out details, and she picked it up to verify.

It was not a photo of Lila. It was a photo of her.

Of *Jessica*.

It had been taken at their wedding, but it must have been a snapshot someone else had taken since Jessica had never seen it and it wasn't by the photographer they'd hired.

She was in her wedding dress and her adorable little fur shrug, and she was laughing and clinging to Daniel's arm.

Most of Daniel was cut out of the picture, but Jessica's face and upper body were framed in the shot.

She looked happy and surprisingly pretty, but her eyes were fixed up on Daniel's face with a look of naked affection.

She flushed, standing alone in the workshop, at how much her expression revealed of her feelings for him.

But then her mind caught up to what she was seeing, and she tried to think through the significance.

What was he doing with her picture out here?

Maybe he kept it to remind himself that she was his wife now and he shouldn't be yearning instead for his dead wife.

Or maybe...

She couldn't let herself hope. Every time she'd started to hope in that direction, she'd been crushed. And it should be more than obvious that Daniel didn't want to give himself to her intimately, emotionally. He'd made that very clear yesterday.

But she was shaky when she carefully returned the picture underneath the hammer, turned off the light, and closed the door.

The wind was even more biting than usual as she trudged back to the house, and her mind and heart were spinning with too much to possibly process.

The phone was ringing when she walked into the house, and she ran for it.

Maybe it was Daniel. Maybe he would say he was sorry.

As soon as she saw the name of her mother's nursing facility on the screen, her heart started to hammer in an entirely different way.

They wouldn't call this early on a Sunday morning unless there was an emergency.

The pounding of her heart moved to her ears as the female voice on the other end explained what had happened. Her mother had fallen. It was serious. They were taking her to the hospital now—the closest one to Willow Park, twenty minutes away.

Jessica had jumped up to grab her keys, and she was out the door before the call was over, before she'd even grabbed a coat.

～

Three hours later, Jessica sat by herself in an otherwise empty waiting area, staring blindly down at the tablet in her lap.

Her mother had broken her hip, and they'd taken her into surgery to try to set it. It wasn't a life-threatening injury, but at her mother's age and state of health, all surgeries were risky.

And it just didn't seem fair that her mother was hit with this on top of everything else.

When Jessica's phone rang, she snatched it up.

"Hey, I just got out of church and got your message. Is your mom okay?" Kim asked, her voice filled with concern.

"I guess." When her voice cracked, Jessica cleared her throat. "She's in surgery. She broke her hip."

"What happened?"

"She fell when she was walking down a few stairs outside at the home."

"Do they think she'll be okay?"

"They said she should be. But everyone looked so concerned. And the surgery seems to be taking so long."

Kim's voice changed. "Are *you* okay?"

"Yeah. I'm fine."

"What are you doing?"

"Just sitting here in the hospital."

"Is Daniel there yet?"

Jessica felt a strange lump in her throat and didn't answer.

"Jess, where is he?"

"He's at church. It's Sunday morning."

"Shit, you didn't even call him, did you?"

Jessica felt so upset and anxious and exhausted that she was just numb. Not even close to tears. "I said I was fine."

"You aren't fine. Are you there all by yourself?"

"There's nothing anyone can do. I'm just sitting here and waiting."

"But you need some support. Why on earth didn't you call Daniel?"

"Because there's nothing he can do. He had to preach this morning. We were fighting last night, and—"

"And that's ridiculous! He'd want to be there. Jess, he needs to know."

"I'll tell him when there's something to tell."

"Do you really think he wouldn't come to be with you?"

"I know he would come, but I don't want him here out of obligation." It seemed important for Jessica to say that. Important that she meant it.

"He's your husband!"

"I know he's my husband." Jessica didn't want to be having this conversation. She didn't have the strength to deal with it. She just wanted to sit in a stupor and try not to think about anything. "But you know it's not a normal marr—"

"I know it's not a normal marriage, but he'd still want to—"

"I don't want him here out of obligation," Jessica repeated, gritting out the words since they were the ones she was surest of. "I don't want him obliged to me."

"*Of course* he's obliged to you. You're friends. You're in a relationship. You're married, for whatever reason. Obligation comes with all that."

"I don't care. I don't want him to do anything for me because he *has* to. Only because he *wants* to." Ridiculously, a tear slipped out of one eye, although she'd thought she was too numb to cry. She didn't even have the energy to wipe it away.

Kim was silent for too long. "I'm really sorry, Jess," she said at last. "I shouldn't be bringing all this up now. But you need someone with you. Is there anyone else?"

"I don't need anyone. I keep telling you. I'm fine."

"I've got a rehearsal I can't miss right now, but then I'll come down. I can be there by midafternoon."

"You don't need to—"

"I don't care what I need to do. I'm doing it anyway."

For no good reason, Jessica's face twisted in emotion. After taking a shaky breath, she said, "Thanks."

After she hung up, she sat with her phone in her hand. Her tablet had gone black from disuse.

If Daniel called, she would tell him. If he called, it would be a gesture that he wasn't closing her out after all. It wasn't like him to give her—or anyone—the cold shoulder. He would wonder why she hadn't showed up for church. He had a Session meeting after the service, but he'd be back home by around one. Then he'd wonder where she was.

Maybe he would think she'd gone somewhere to pout by herself, but maybe he'd feel bad and call to make peace.

Either way, she wasn't going to call him. She knew what he would do. He would drop everything and come out to the hospital to be with her. He'd be strong and comforting and supportive.

And he'd do it all out of nothing but duty, when she wanted so much more from him.

She'd thought she was getting everything she really wanted in this marriage, but she'd been wrong. She wanted—needed—a lot more.

She shook the thought from her mind since Daniel wasn't the most important thing right now.

Her mother was the most important thing.

And it felt like every day she was slipping further away from her.

Another tear streamed down her cheek, and this time she managed to swipe it away.

"Jessica, are you okay?"

Her head jerked up at the unexpected voice, and she saw an elderly woman with a sympathetic smile extending a cup of coffee to her.

Without thinking, Jessica took the coffee and then the sugar and creamer packets. "Yeah."

Randa Verbois, who'd lived in Willow Park all her life and who volunteered at the hospital a couple of times a week, sat down in the chair next to her. "How's your mother?"

"She's in surgery." Jessica busied herself with putting creamer in the coffee and stirring it more than it needed stirring. "I don't know anything yet."

"Is there anything I can do, dear?"

Randa had taught her Sunday school. She was allowed to call her "dear."

"No, but thank you."

"When is Pastor Daniel going to get here?"

Jessica felt suddenly trapped. "I… uh, I'm not sure."

"Well, you let me know if you need anything before he does."

"Thank you." Jessica smiled at the woman, despite her awkwardness.

Of course Randa assumed Daniel would be coming. He was her husband.

No one but Kim knew the truth.

~

A half hour later, nothing had changed except Jessica had finished her cup of coffee.

She still held her phone in her hand, but it hadn't rung. Her tablet still rested on her lap, but she hadn't turned it back on.

Her mother was still in surgery, and no one had come with any news.

Jessica tried to pray, tried to be as reasonable as she'd always been about life. It was just a broken hip. They did this surgery all the time. Everything would be okay.

Despite her best efforts, she kept imagining how she would feel if something happened to her mother.

If her mom died, then Jessica would have no one. No family left. She would be as alone as she'd ever been in her life.

This marriage was supposed to keep that from happening, but it hadn't. It hadn't changed anything at all.

Her shoulders shook, and she fought the rising emotion in her chest and throat.

"Jessica," a familiar voice said.

For a moment, she was so numb she thought the voice was in her head.

"Jessica," the voice said again. Closer now. Then someone took four long steps toward her and sank into the chair beside her. He took both of her hands in his. "Is she okay?"

Jessica stared at Daniel blankly, trying to get her mind to work.

"Jessica, honey, is she okay?"

"I don't know. She's in surgery."

He released her hands and moved his warm hands up to her face. "Are *you* okay?"

"I'm fin—" She couldn't finish the lie. She broke down into tight little sobs.

She had no idea what Daniel was doing here now, but she was so, so glad to see him.

He made a wordless, guttural sound and pulled her into a hug. It was slightly awkward since they had to hug over the armrest between them, but she didn't care.

She cried into his shoulder for a minute or two, feeling safe and cared for as his arms held her tightly.

Finally, she pulled away, wiping her eyes and feeling kind of silly, but much better than she had before.

"What are you doing here?" she asked, rubbing her face. She must look horrible. She was still wearing her church clothes, but her eyes must be swollen and red, and she'd pulled her hair back in a messy ponytail to keep it out of her way.

"Randa called. She was worried about you, and she wanted to make sure I was on my way." His eyes bore into her, as if searching for something in her expression. "She assumed I already knew."

"I know she did."

"Why didn't you tell me?" The words weren't accusatory. Just bewildered.

She looked away. "I don't know."

"Did you think I wouldn't care? I'm so sorry about last night, and I shouldn't have left this morning without putting things right between us, but did you really think I wouldn't care that your—"

"I knew you would care. It wasn't that."

"Then what was it?"

She shrugged and couldn't meet his eyes. She couldn't tell him the truth—that she wanted his love and would never get it. So there was no good answer she could give.

"Jessica?" he prompted.

She just shrugged again. "I just didn't."

He didn't push the issue, perhaps recognizing that she wasn't in a fit state to talk about it. "Did you get any lunch?"

"I'm not hungry."

"Well, you have to eat something."

"I said I'm not—"

"Then you can come watch me eat."

"I'm not going to leave—"

"We'll just go down to the cafeteria. We'll ask Randa to call if there's any news. But the surgery takes a long time, and you'll feel better if you don't sit and brood."

"I wasn't brooding." Her objection was mostly out of principle since she *had* been brooding and there was no reason not to go down to the cafeteria. She stood up, went to the bathroom, washed her face, and got onto the elevator with him. In the cafeteria, she ate half a sandwich, which made her stomach feel better since all she'd had since that morning were four cups of coffee.

An hour later, they were back in the waiting area on a row of chairs without armrests. Daniel had his arm around her, and she was leaning against him.

"Why is it taking so long?" she mumbled, readjusting to get more comfortable and in the process wrapping an arm around his waist.

His head moved against hers, and she was almost sure he pressed a kiss into her hair. "It's a complicated procedure, I think, but they do it all the time. I'm sure she'll be fine."

Jessica sighed. Then she glanced up at his face, catching a look that startled her since it was so full of tender feeling. "You don't have to stay here all afternoon with me."

His expression transformed into surprised annoyance. "You think I'm going to leave you?"

"No, I'm just saying you don't have to stay. I know you must be tired after preaching this morning, and you didn't get much sleep last night, and there's nothing here for—"

"I'm not going to leave you here alone."

"I know I was pitiful earlier, but I'm really okay. You don't have to feel sor—"

"I don't feel sorry for you. I want to be here. So stop trying to get me to leave."

"I'm not trying to get you to leave. I just don't want you to feel oblige—"

He groaned and rubbed his face with one hand. "I know I've made a mess of our relationship lately. I know it's my fault. But I would have been here for you before we got married, just because we're friends. Why would you think I'd do any less now that you're my wife?"

For some reason, the earnestness of the words made her cheeks flush. "Okay," she mumbled, leaning against him again, mostly to hide her expression.

He wrapped his arm around her once more, and they sat together in silence.

When Randa walked by a few minutes later, she smiled at them maternally, evidently feeling like she'd accomplished a job well done.

∼

Jessica was gently shaken awake by a hand on her shoulder.

She blinked up, gradually recognizing Daniel's face above her. Her head hurt, and her back hurt, and she had no idea where she was.

"It's late," Daniel said, kneeling down beside her chair. "Do you want to go home?"

Jessica blinked a few more times, realizing she was in the hospital room with her mother. Her eyes flew to her mom, who was asleep on her bed. She was hooked up to all kinds of devices, but she seemed to be resting comfortably.

"I don't know." Her voice was scratchy, and she couldn't get her mind to work. "What time is it?"

"After ten."

The afternoon had been a blur. Her mom had gotten out of surgery about the time that Kim had arrived. Kim had stayed for several hours, letting Daniel go back and let Bear out and keep a counseling appointment he'd scheduled.

He'd come back around afterward, bringing some takeout for dinner. Kim had left then, and they'd stayed with her mom in the room until Jessica fell asleep.

Daniel stood up and helped her to her feet. "Why don't you walk a little and stretch out? Then you can figure out what you want to do."

She nodded, relieved to stretch out the knot in her back. Daniel put a strong arm around her as they walked down the empty hallway.

Jessica stopped by the bathroom and threw water on her face, and she felt a little better although her head still ached.

Daniel was leaning against the wall when she came out of the bathroom. He'd taken off the jacket to his suit and his tie earlier in the day, and his trousers and dress shirt were wrinkled. His jaw looked more scraggly than usual, and his eyes were tired and so tender they took her breath away.

Without thinking, responding only to the look in his eyes, she walked over to him, reaching up to wrap her arms around his neck and press her body against his.

He slid his arms around her and held her to him in a hug.

"Are you all right?" he asked eventually, murmuring the words against her ear.

"Yeah." Her voice was muffled because her mouth was still against his shirt.

"What do you want to do, honey?" He adjusted so both of his hands were at the small of her back. "I'll stay with you if you don't want to leave her, but I think you'd feel a lot better if you went home to get some sleep. She seems to be okay for now."

"Yeah," Jessica murmured, so exhausted she could barely move. "Let's go home."

Before they could move, a voice came from farther down the hall. "What are y'all doing? Making out in the middle of the hospital?"

Jessica straightened up, startled by the interruption to their innocent embrace, and Daniel let his arms drop to his side.

Micah approached, giving them a questioning grin.

"What are you doing here?" Daniel asked his brother.

"Hello to you too." Micah turned to Jessica. "How's your mom?"

"She's okay. She's sleeping."

"Seriously, what are you doing here so late?" Daniel prompted.

"Just checking on you all. Are you going to stay here all night? Do you want me to stop by and let the dog out?"

"Bear," Jessica put in.

"Sorry. Bear." Micah really was a good-looking guy, casual and masculine in jeans and a flannel shirt. She figured all the girls in town must be after him. He used to be pretty wild, but Daniel said he hadn't really dated since he'd come back to the church.

"No. We were about to head home." Daniel put a hand on the small of her back and nudged her forward. "Thanks though. You didn't have to come all the way out here."

"Not a problem. I've always liked your mom." He gave Jessica an ironic half smile. "She made the best caramel corn."

"No argument here," Daniel agreed with a smile in his voice. "Although Jessica can make it just as good."

~

An hour later, Jessica crawled into bed feeling like she'd been through a battle.

Daniel's truck wouldn't start in the hospital parking lot, even though he and Micah had spent about fifteen minutes fiddling with the engine. So Daniel had driven her home in her car, saying he'd deal with the truck in the morning.

Jessica had taken a shower, but that was all she had energy to do. Daniel had taken Bear out on a short walk, but now he was in the shower too.

The light at his bedside was on, so she could see him clearly as he came into the bedroom wearing only a pair of pajama pants, which was his normal sleeping attire even in the winter.

His body was gorgeous, but she didn't even have energy to leer tonight.

"I thought you might already be asleep," he said, climbing into bed beside her.

"Not yet."

He reached out to draw her into his arms.

She went willingly, loving the feel of his warm, strong body beside hers. But she mumbled, "I don't think I'm up to sex tonight."

He made a gruff sound in his throat. "Do you really think I'm going to make a move on you tonight?"

"Oh." She shifted enough to look up at his face.

His expression softened. "I was just going to hold you."

"Oh. That's okay, then." It's was more than okay. It was exactly what she wanted. Needed. She snuggled against him.

He stroked her hair and rubbed her back, and she sighed as her body relaxed.

"I'm sorry I didn't call you right away," she mumbled after a few minutes. "After I found out about Mom, I mean."

Daniel didn't answer right away. "That's okay. I understand why you didn't."

She felt better with her apology given and accepted, so she sighed again.

Then he said, "I almost called you about twenty times this morning, wanting to apologize."

For some reason, her heartbeat sped up. "Why didn't you?"

"Because I'm an idiot."

"Oh. I already knew that."

He gave a huff of amusement, and his arm tightened around her. "I really am sorry. About yesterday. And everything. I know I was shutting you out, and I know it wasn't right."

"I know it's hard for you," she said, feeling safer because it was dark, because she wasn't looking at his face, and because his arm was holding her close. "It's okay. I understand. But we can't... we can't make this work if you close me out."

"I know."

When he didn't say anything else, she swallowed hard. "Do you... do you *want* this to work?"

"Of course I do." He answered immediately, no hesitation in his voice.

She had to believe him.

"Then we'll keep working on it," she said.

"Yeah. We'll keep working on it.

# TEN

"I'm serious, Jessica. You've been here all day."

Jessica sighed and looked up at her husband, who was standing over her and frowning in concern. "I'm fine. I want to be with my mom. What's so wrong with that?"

"Nothing is wrong with it in theory. But you got here at eight this morning, and it's now after five. It's not good for you to just sit here all day."

Her mom was doing as expected today, just a day after the surgery. She'd been sleeping most of the day. "I don't want to leave her alone. I'm all she has."

Daniel squatted down next to her chair so he was closer to her eye level. "Randa is here this evening. She said she'd sit with her as much as she can. She's just sleeping now anyway."

Jessica glanced back over to the bed. Her mother would be in the hospital for a while. Then she'd get moved into rehab. Then she'd get moved back into the home.

Not a very promising future.

Not much of a future at all.

"Jessica," Daniel said, his voice thicker now. He took her face in his hand to turn her back to look at him. "She's okay right now. And you staying here isn't going to make it all better."

She swallowed hard. "I know."

"You need to take care of yourself too."

"I know." She hadn't eaten much today. She was starving.

"Honey," he said, taking her face in both of his hands, "You need to let someone help you sometimes."

"I do let people help me." Her voice was wavering since she was so affected by Daniel's voice and his intense expression. He'd only called her "honey" a couple of times, but she loved the sound of it. She wasn't sure he was even conscious of doing it.

"No, you really don't."

"I do."

"Okay. So you do. This is me, helping you."

A shudder of emotion ran through her. "Okay."

He blinked. "Okay?"

"Okay."

"Okay what?" He still looked a little suspicious at her acquiescence. "Okay, you'll let me take you home?"

She nodded.

His face reflected relief, and he stood up and then helped her to feet.

"I've got to do the intro to the choir concert at church this evening," he said after she'd kissed her mom's cheek and they were on their way out, "but I don't have to stay for the concert, so I'll only be gone for fifteen minutes or so."

"You should stay for the whole thing. I don't want people to think I'm falling apart."

"They're not going to think you're falling apart. They'll think I want to be with my wife when she needs me."

"I'm really okay. It's my mom who has had the rough time. I actually kind of want to go to the concert."

He looked surprised as he opened the passenger door to her car, which they were sharing since he'd had to take his old truck to the shop—the repairs beyond his and Micah's abilities. "I know, but I thought you'd be too tired to go."

"I don't know. I'm kind of tired, but I hate to miss it. I've gone every single year of my life."

"I know." He shut the door for her and walked around to the driver's side. "Me too. We can go, if you want."

"I think I do, unless I'm too tired when I get home."

Daniel drove to a chain restaurant near the hospital so they could get something to eat, and she ate the burger and fries gratefully. They didn't talk much, but it didn't feel like they needed to.

When she got home, she laid down for about a half hour and dozed off. When she woke up, she felt better, and there was still time for her to get dressed before the concert, so she decided she wanted to go after all. Everyone always dressed up for the yearly Christmas choir concert, so she showered quickly and put on something nice—a straight skirt and a dark red velvet top.

She was doing her makeup when Daniel came into the bathroom to brush his teeth.

"Don't get toothpaste on your tie," she chided, holding his tie back from the sink when he leaned over to spit.

He frowned at her, but she knew it wasn't from genuine annoyance.

Then she glanced down at the tie, which was still in her hand. She smiled in surprise. "I got you this tie last Christmas." It was festive without being gaudy in dark red, green, and gold stripes.

"I know you did."

She felt a shiver at the textured sound of his voice, but she tried not to blow it out of proportion. He liked to take care of people. He cared about her.

It didn't necessarily mean anything significant between them had changed.

"You look beautiful."

"I do not." She looked at herself in the mirror. She did look nice, she thought. The red color brought out the color in her cheeks and made her eyes look very blue. It also flattered her figure, which was unusual since she normally wore baggy sweatshirts.

"Yes, you do. Do you have to argue with everything I say?"

"I only argue when you're wrong."

He chuckled. "I don't think I'm wrong quite as often as you argue with me. And I know I'm not wrong about this. You look absolutely breathtaking."

"Oh." She wanted to squirm in pleasure but managed to resist the impulse. "Thank you."

To distract herself from sappy feelings, she brushed a couple of white hairs off his trousers. "You've been petting Bear."

"I have not been petting that dog. She gets more than enough attention from you."

Jessica giggled. "I saw you petting her earlier."

"See. What did I say about your always arguing with me?"

"Well, that's not my fault. You keep being wrong."

~

The concert was at the church, which was decorated beautifully for the Christmas season with wreaths, poinsettias, and candles and garlands at the windows.

Despite being rather tired, Jessica couldn't help but feel a thrill of appreciation for the old sanctuary, for the season, for the familiar faces gathered for a concert she'd gone to every year of her life. It made her feel connected to the people, the traditions, a long history, the community. It was the kind of feeling she'd been seeking but not feeling all the time the way she'd wanted.

Daniel's only duty was to open the concert with a short welcome and say a prayer before it got started. She felt a different sort of thrill as she watched him greet the congregation with his usual warm charisma—that he was hers more than anyone else's.

He came back to sit beside her when he'd finished, and he put his arm around her shoulders casually as the first song began.

It wasn't anything intimate or inappropriate. It just felt natural. It just felt like they were a couple.

A real couple. Not a strange, pragmatically half-married couple.

For the first time in their marriage, she didn't immediately try to talk herself out of the idea.

It wasn't just her imagination. She knew something had changed yesterday. He hadn't pulled back immediately afterward, the way he always had after they'd been close before. He'd made some sort of genuine emotional commitment. To her. To their marriage. Not just that he'd be faithful and hold up his end of the bargain, but that he would try to genuinely be *with* her.

It was impossible not to see the difference.

It was what she wanted—so close to what she wanted. It made her happy. Hopeful. That one day he might love her the way she loved him.

Perhaps because of this realization, or perhaps because she was so incredibly tired after a really long weekend, as the concert progressed, she got more and more emotional.

She couldn't seem to control it, although she didn't know of any reason for the excessive emotion. When the audience stood for the Hallelujah Chorus, which concluded the concert every year, tears slipped from her eyes.

It was embarrassing. She was never like this. She'd never been one of those women who cried at the drop of a hat. She kept trying to discreetly wipe the tears away, but they kept coming anyway.

After a minute, Daniel wrapped an arm around her, and she hid her face against his shoulder, shaking just a little.

"You okay?" he murmured, his mouth just next to her ear.

"Yeah."

"Anything I need to know?"

"No." She managed to look up at him. "I'm just emotional. It's stupid."

He peered at her face closely, as if searching for whether she'd told him the truth. Evidently satisfied, he pressed his lips softly against hers. "I don't think you're stupid."

"Now who's arguing all the time? Anyway, it's disrespectful to kiss during the Hallelujah Chorus. Pay attention." She was pleased her voice was light and teasing, although she was feeling anything but.

"Right," he said with a twitch of a smile, turning back to the choir.

She was giddy—no other word for it—as she listened to the last triumphant bars, the music somehow matching the joyful swell of her heart.

They stayed for the reception afterward, and she was overwhelmed by the outpouring of concern for her as people gathered to ask about her mother and whether they could do anything to help.

She was so surprised and disoriented that she wasn't prepared when the conversation turned to the choir and Daniel said casually, "Jessica is thinking about joining."

She gasped and poked him in the side.

He blinked down at her in feigned surprise. "You said you were thinking about it."

She gave him a discreet glare since he'd obviously made the public statement on purpose.

"Oh, you *must* join," Martha said. "You have such a lovely voice. We need another alto."

"I'm thinking about it."

"Just come and try it out to see if you like it. You don't have to commit."

"I'm thinking about it." In the face of all those expectant eyes, she said, "I'll come a couple of times in January to see if I like it."

Then she poked Daniel in the side again since he was looking far too pleased with himself.

"Ouch."

Those around them laughed at this bit of byplay, and Jessica pretended to laugh too.

As they were leaving, Daniel asked, "Did you mean it about trying out for the choir?"

"Yes. I wouldn't have said it if I didn't mean it."

"Good. Are you upset about it?"

"Why have you gotten it in your head that I should do this?"

He was looking baffled and concerned by her shift in mood. "I think you'll like it."

Her giddiness had taken a hit from the possible explanation that occurred to her. Normally, she wouldn't have admitted to it since it revealed too much about her own feelings, but she didn't have enough defenses to hold it back tonight. "Do you think I need to do the choir? As part of being your wife?"

Daniel stopped in the middle of the parking lot, a few flakes of blowing snow landing on his dark hair before they melted. "What?"

"You seem to be pushing the idea so hard, and I wondered if you thought I needed to be more involved in the church—as a pastor's wife, I mean. If that's the case, it would just be easier if you came out and told me how much you need me to do."

Daniel almost choked on visible shock. "Of course you don't have to do anything because you're my wife. I'd never expect you to do anything for reasons like that."

He seemed so authentically surprised—almost indignant—at the idea that she had to believe him. "Oh," she said.

"Jessica." He reached out to put a hand on her shoulder. "I don't have a picture in my mind of the kind of wife you're supposed to be. I don't care if you cook or sing in the choir or do anything but be yourself. Don't do any of those things for me, because you think that's the kind of wife I want."

She felt strange, shaky. "Then why are you pushing the choir so much?"

"Because I think you'd really enjoy it. Because I think it might help you feel more connected, and you said that's what you want." He reached up and cupped her cheek with one big hand. "Honey, I want you to have everything out of life that you want."

She swayed toward him, drawn by the naked affection in his eyes. "And you really think the choir is the way to get there?"

"I don't know. But I know you can't get connected the way you want until you take a risk, until you put yourself out there. I know that's hard for you—it's hard for everyone—but I thought the choir might be a small risk you could take that might pay off. If you really don't want to do it, I'll drop it for good. But I thought you were just afraid."

"I was," she admitted. "I am. But I can try it. Maybe I'll like it."

He smiled in obvious satisfaction. "Good."

"All I said was that I'd try it out. So if I don't like it, you can't complain if I quit."

"I won't complain. But I don't think you're going to quit."

She grumbled under her breath, but mostly just for show.

They walked the rest of the way to the car, and he opened the passenger door for her. "Are you tired?"

"Not too tired. Why?"

"We could get some dessert if you want. The cookies there left something to be desired."

"You don't really think I'm going to turn down dessert, do you?"

They went to a coffee shop on Main Street. They knew almost everyone in the place when they walked in, about half the patrons having come from the concert just like them.

They said hello to everyone they knew and then picked out cupcakes from the case. She got red velvet, and he got carrot. Daniel got regular coffee, and she got decaf.

There was one tiny table open in the far corner. She glanced over at it and then up at Daniel.

"It's kind of stuffy in here," he said. "Is it too chilly to go outside?"

"It's not too bad. We can go out if you want."

They went down the block to the duck pond and found a bench. It was chilly, but not unbearably so. They both had coats on, and Jessica leaned again Daniel, who was always warm.

She smiled up at him as she took a bite of her cupcake.

It was so strange. Almost like they were on a date.

The thought made her feel ridiculously shy, so she kept her eyes on her cupcake, licking the cream cheese icing off her fingers as she ate.

It kept feeling like Daniel was looking at her though, so she finally glanced up to see.

When she saw his eyes were indeed resting on her, she asked, "Do I have icing on my face?"

"A little," he murmured, reaching over and swiping the corner of her lip with his thumb.

For some reason, the little gesture made her shiver.

"Is it gone?" she asked, trying to sound natural and not like she was about to melt into the bench.

"Just about." He rubbed her lip with his thumb again, but his time it was more like a caress.

She couldn't look away from his eyes. She was trapped by the expression.

When the shivery sensation from the pad of his thumb on her lip started to generate different kinds of feelings, running down her spine and even lower, she dropped her head backward and sucked in a breath.

"You're so beautiful," Daniel murmured, sliding his thumb from her lip to her cheek and then back.

"That's what you said before."

"Well, I meant it then. And I mean it now."

She felt like she might melt into a hot puddle of feeling. "Do you?"

"Look at me, honey. Then tell me you don't believe me."

She managed to focus on his face again, and she gasped at the expression in his eyes. It was heated, possessive, so much more than admiring. It looked like he wanted to swallow her whole.

"Do you believe me?" he asked, low and thick.

"Yeah."

"Good." Then he tilted his head down to kiss her.

She responded immediately, couldn't help but respond. A rush of pleasure and emotion rose up as he moved his lips against hers, sliding his tongue into her mouth.

She clutched at his shoulders with one hand, still trying to hold her cupcake with the other.

She was just getting into it when a voice broke into the fog of sensation.

"I'm shocked!" a booming voice said from behind them. "The pastor making out in public! Such a bad example for the youth in the town."

They broke apart, and Jessica turned her head to see the grinning face of one of the church deacons, who was walking by with his wife. Both were laughing with genuine warmth.

Irrationally embarrassed, Jessica dropped her face to Daniel's shoulder.

He said, "I'm more than happy to set an example of making out with one's wife—at any time or place."

They all laughed, and the other couple kept walking. When they were out of earshot, Daniel grumbled, "We'd have to leave the county to get any privacy around here."

Jessica giggled. "Or we could just go home."

"Yeah," he said, a hot promise in his eyes. "Let's go home."

∼

They were kissing again as they unlocked the door. And kissing as they let Bear outside in the backyard for a minute.

And kissing as they stumbled upstairs. And kissing as they tumbled into their bed, already trying to pull off each other's clothes.

She'd made quick work of his shirt, and they both were trying to pull off his trousers, but they got hung up on his shoes, which he'd never taken off.

It was a bit of a kerfuffle, causing them to laugh as they finally managed to get the shoes and pants off, but then Daniel wasted no time in moving on top of her.

"I don't know what's wrong with me," he said, pushing up her skirt and moving aside her panties. "I've never been like this in my life."

"Like what?" she managed to ask, after gasping as he nudged her entrance. She was already aroused just from their clumsy, half-interrupted foreplay.

"Like I'm a horny teenager, unable to think about anything except how much I want you all the time." He groaned as he sank inside her, and she bent her knees to give him better access.

"You do?"

He'd closed his eyes, his expression reflecting pleasure and hunger both. But now he opened them again. "I do what?"

"You think about wanting me all the time?" She tangled her fingers in his hair, feeling so much more than the familiar tightness of having him inside her.

"Of course I do. Don't you know that? I've never been like this before. It's almost embarrassing."

She arched in pleasure, from his words even more than the sensation of him starting to move inside her. She knew what he was saying—even obliquely.

He wanted her in a different way than he'd ever wanted Lila.

There was part of him that could be distinctly hers.

She'd never dreamed it was possible, and it intensified the physical sensations.

When he began to thrust, she moved with him, rocking up her hips, huffing out little panting sounds.

"Oh, honey, you feel so good." He ducked his head for a minute, his hips working fast and hard between her thighs. "You always feel so good."

She made a sobbing sound as so much—too much—overwhelmed her all at once.

She shook her hips desperately as the pleasure coiled into a tight knot. Then cried out loudly as it released.

He was with her, his extended exclamation just as helpless as hers.

She gathered him to her afterward, stroking his back, murmuring out incoherent words of affection and release.

When he finally raised his head to look down at her, she was relieved that there was no shadow in his eyes. They were just as warm as they'd been before—but relaxed instead of urgent.

"We're pretty good together," she said, raising her hand to stroke his rough face, loving the feel of his beard against her palm. "At least, I think so."

He gave a huff of ironic laughter. "I think saying we're good together is a massive understatement."

She grinned up at him, the flood of joy impossible to stop. "We're good together outside the bedroom too, I think."

To her relief, he showed no sign of withdrawing, despite the intimacy of the words. He leaned down to kiss her softly. "We're very good together. In every way."

"I think so too."

"This marriage was a very good idea."

It might not be a declaration of love, but it was more than Jessica had ever thought to hear from him.

~

Jessica woke up in the middle of the night and rolled over toward Daniel's side. Even mostly asleep, she was conscious of a bleak expectation of finding his side empty.

Instead, her arm landed on his chest as she rolled.

He grunted at the impact.

"Sorry," she said, too groggy to process anything but the relief that he was still in bed with her.

"What's... matter?" he mumbled.

"Nothing. It was an accident."

"'Kay." He seemed mostly asleep, but he moved her body until she was lying beside him instead of half on top of him.

This seemed a perfectly good arrangement as far as Jessica was concerned, so she curled up beside him and went back to sleep.

# ELEVEN

When she woke up, she was still beside Daniel—so cozy she was almost too warm.

Her cheek was pressed up against his chest, and she pulled away from it and rolled away, inhaling a thick breath.

When she glanced over at the clock, she saw it was just after five.

When she glanced up at his face, she saw he was awake.

"Hi," she said, self-conscious since he seemed to have been watching her while she slept.

"Hi."

"How long have you been awake?"

"About a half hour."

"You didn't want to get up and take your run?"

He gave her a half smile. "I guess I'm lazy today."

"I don't think it's lazy to want to stay in bed past five on Christmas Eve morning."

"I'm glad to have your approval."

Feeling a surge of affection, she scooted back over, settling herself beside him and wrapping an arm around his middle.

He adjusted to put an arm around her.

"What were you thinking about, lying in bed all this time?" she asked, caressing his belly with her palm.

"I was praying."

"Oh. I won't disturb you then. Sorry."

"Don't be."

He didn't say any more, but he'd brought the subject up, so after a minute she found the courage to ask, "Do you... do you feel any better... about things, I mean."

Despite her vague question, he evidently knew exactly what she was talking about. "I've been working through some things."

"I know you have."

"Lila was in the accident in December."

"I know she was." Two years ago. Jessica hadn't been as close to Daniel then, but it had still hit her hard. One morning the woman had been alive, and by the end of the day she was dead. No warning. No preparation. Just dead in the space of a minute.

"I thought I'd processed everything, grieved for her, reconciled myself. I thought I was recovered until this last month."

"I don't think grief ever really gets put behind you for good. I think it's normal that you'd still miss her, that you'd still wish she were here." It hurt a little to say so since she liked the idea of Daniel loving no one but her. But that was a petty, immature response, so she wasn't going to indulge it.

He stroked her hair back from her face. "Yeah, but that's not what I've been going through. I do still miss her sometimes, but this hasn't been grief. Maybe it looks like it, but it isn't."

She'd been resting her head on his chest but now she raised it to search his face. "It isn't?"

He shook his head. "It's all been spiritual. You know that much, I think. But I don't want you to think I'm wrestling with God this way because I still want Lila. I don't want you to ever believe that I want you to be her. Because I don't."

Jessica took a shaky breath and tried to think of a response. There was nothing. She wasn't sure she was capable of shaping a word anyway. She'd needed so much to hear that. Needed so much to know it.

"It's not all better or anything," he added. "But I hope I'm making progress. I just wanted you to know."

She pressed a soft kiss on his chest and managed to say, "Thank you."

They lay in silence for a few minutes. Then Daniel said, "Sometimes I wonder what the church would think if they knew how messed up I am."

She scowled at him. "That's ridiculous. You *know* that's ridiculous."

"Yeah. I guess." He sounded almost resigned.

She raised herself up, supported by straightened arms. "Anyone who thinks a pastor has it all together has never met one."

"Thanks a lot."

"You know what I mean. The point of faith is that you don't need to have it all together. You know that. You've told me that yourself."

"I know. But it's easier to say it when you feel like you're on the right track."

"You *are* on the right track, Daniel. So get over your insufferable arrogance and admit that you struggle just as much as anyone else."

To her surprise, his mouth quirked up. "You're getting rather bossy, you know."

She tried to smother the laughter that rippled out of her, relieved that Daniel's characteristic dry humor had returned. "I am not bossy. And you shouldn't be calling me that. I'm your wife, and you should only be speaking sweet words about me."

He burst into laughter and pulled her into a hug, rolling them over so he was on top of her. "That sounded rather bossy to me."

"You have a skewed frame of reference when it comes to bossiness. That was simply a statement of fact."

"It was a fact?"

"Yes. It's a fact that husbands should speak only sweet things about their wives." She thought she did pretty well about keeping her tone serious, even as she was shaking with amusement.

"Oh, okay. I'll give it a try. Hmm. My wife..."

She waited breathlessly, overwhelmed by the teasing warmth in his eyes. When he didn't continue, she swatted him on the shoulder. "Well?"

He chuckled. "My wife has the most beautiful eyes I've ever seen."

She couldn't hide a rather besotted grin. "Well, that was pretty good for a start."

"More? All right. My wife... can make me laugh more than anyone I've ever known."

Her laughter faded into a rise of emotion as she processed what he'd said.

His eyes were still warm, but they weren't as teasing anymore. "And my wife has a remarkable mind. And a remarkable heart. And she takes my breath away every time she finds the courage to take a risk and tell me the truth."

His voice cracked on the last word, and there was a lump in Jessica's throat too.

They stared at each other for a long moment.

Then she whispered, "I do?"

He leaned down to kiss her. "You do."

Afraid she was going to get swept away in sentiment, she managed to regain enough irony to say, "I guess that was a pretty good start at sweetness. You'll have to keep practicing."

"Who said I was done?"

"There's more? I'm all ears."

He hid a smile. "My wife has the most... annoying dog I've ever—"

His drawled words broke off abruptly when Jessica gave a cry of outrage and tried to push him off her.

They had a brief, laughing wrestling match until Daniel gave up in mock surrender. "Fine. My wife has a dog who is just as sweet as she is."

She frowned. "I think that was rather backhanded as far as sweet words go."

"Nope. Nothing backhanded about it."

They lay smiling at each other until he asked, "So husbands don't get sweet words too?"

"Only if they're really good."

"Ah. Then no sweet words for me."

"Right."

"Too bad."

She scooted over to kiss him. "My husband is smarter and hotter than any man I know."

He looked surprised—but very pleased—by the compliment, so she kissed him again.

Then she added, "And his heart is so incredibly kind… to everyone except himself."

~

They had to get up soon afterward since they had to go to church as the team was meeting to take the canned and dry goods from the Christmas drive to the local food pantry.

Jessica took Bear for a walk while Daniel showered and dressed, and then Jessica got ready while he did his devotions and cleared out some e-mail.

When she was ready early, Jessica felt a burst of energy and mixed up some muffin mix out of a box. She was just pulling the muffins out of the oven when Daniel came into the kitchen, wearing jeans and a college sweatshirt.

"Yum," he said, grabbing one from the tray.

"Wait, they're hot!"

He broke the muffin open, letting out a burst of steam. "I can blow on it."

She narrowed her eyes as he blew with exaggerated force on the muffin half.

He took a bite. "My wife… makes great muffins out of a box."

"How did you know they were out of a box?"

He grinned and nodded toward the trash, where the box was clearly displayed.

"Oh. I'm going to work on baking from scratch. I just haven't had time yet."

"Muffins from a box are better than no muffins at all."

"Keep it up, and you're going to get no muffins."

He laughed, and he looked so adorable that she gooched his sides.

He huffed in surprise, which made her gooch him again.

This time, he grabbed her wrists and turned her around so he had her trapped against the counter.

"I wasn't doing anything," she insisted, widening her eyes with what she hoped was an innocent look.

"You certainly *were* doing something." Then his expression changed. So quickly it stole her breath. He didn't move back, so she could feel his hard body pressed against hers. His brown eyes had grown sober. "Seriously though, Jessica."

She drew her brows together. "Yes, seriously I was gooching you. Is that a problem?"

He gave a bark of laughter. "No. Gooch away. I had switched topics."

"Oh. To what?"

"I just wanted to make sure you're really all right with this."

"With what?" For some reason, her heart started pounding in a way it hadn't all morning. With fear. Or dread. Or *something*.

"With this marriage. Our situation. I think what we have is good and can get even better, but I can't help but feel like I'm getting the better end of the deal. I get the perfect wife—"

"Ha! I'm far from the perfect wife."

"All right, I get exactly what I want and need in a wife, while you get…"

"A very good husband." She was worried now, and her blood was throbbing with her heartbeat, suddenly afraid she was about to hear something heartbreaking.

He was searching her face urgently now, as if trying to read her mind. "And that's enough? What I can offer you? I'm not going to pull away from you again, and I'm as committed to this, to *you*, as anything. But it's not everything you deserve. I can't give you everything, so you're really just getting half a man. Is it really enough for you, not having a love marriage?"

And there was the heartbreaking thing.

She froze—maybe just for a few seconds but it felt like an eternity. Then she took a shuddering breath that was one of the hardest things she'd ever done.

She'd always known what this marriage was about. Daniel had never lied to her about it.

She'd simply lied to herself.

But this was what she'd signed up for, and she'd gotten everything she'd wanted out of it. She had a husband, a partner, companionship, security, the chance at a family.

Expecting something more—wanting something more—wasn't fair to Daniel. Or herself. She couldn't tell him. She couldn't strip herself naked and expose her heart, when she knew her feelings weren't reciprocated.

It might feel wrong, but it wasn't wrong. She'd gotten exactly what she'd asked for.

"Yeah," she said, hoping her voice sounded natural. "I like what we have. It's enough."

She must have come across as convincing, because Daniel relaxed visibly. He leaned down to give her a gentle kiss.

"Okay. We better get going."

"Sounds good," she said, faking a bright smile. "I'm ready to go."

She spent the few hours, as they packed up the food and drove it over to the food bank, convincing herself she had nothing to be depressed about.

This marriage had already given her a lot.

This marriage had never been about love.

∼

They had lunch with her mother at the nursing home and then an early dinner with Micah and Daniel's parents. They were acting like a family. It felt exactly like they were a family. And for some reason, it made Jessica feel even worse.

Daniel was friendly and affectionate all day—the way she'd always wanted him to act. But even that made her feel worse.

She just didn't know why he couldn't love her.

As she was showering and dressing for the Christmas Eve service at church, she felt like she might cry. Right in the middle of putting on one of her socks, she bent over and had to stifle a sudden rise of tears.

"What's the matter, honey?" Daniel said from the doorway of the bathroom. He had a toothbrush in his mouth, so his words were mumbled.

She wished he wouldn't call her "honey." It sounded like he loved her, so it just twisted the knife of reality. "Nothing," she said, straightening up.

He spit out his toothpaste, rinsed for about two seconds, and then came over to sit next to her on the bed. "What's the matter?"

"Nothing."

"I don't believe you. You've gotten really quiet today. Something is bothering you."

"It's nothing important. Silly stuff."

"Well, I care about silly stuff too, so I want to know."

She opened her mouth to tell him but then shut it again.

She wanted to take a risk, to tell him the truth, to let him know she thought something wasn't right in this. She wanted to say that they both needed more than they had.

Maybe some women could tell a man she loved him, without his saying it first, but Jessica wasn't one of those women.

She just couldn't do it. Not when she already knew he didn't love her back.

She closed her mouth and shook her head.

He raised her chin and met her eyes. "You can tell me anything, you know."

She cleared her throat. "I know."

"But you aren't going to tell me this?"

She shook her head, any words she might have said sticking in her throat.

His eyes urgently searched her face. "Will you tell me later?"

"Yeah," she said, mostly just to get him to leave her alone. "Probably later."

This seemed to satisfy him. He got up and glanced at his watch. "You'd better hurry. We need to be over there in twenty minutes."

"Yeah." She hurriedly put on her second sock and then both of her shoes. "Would you mind feeding Bear? I still have to do something with my face."

He rolled his eyes and gave his head a bewildered shake. "Your face is perfect."

That should have made her happy, but it didn't. So she felt even heavier as she put on some mascara and lip gloss and then pulled on a dark green cashmere sweater over her top.

As she went downstairs, she heard Daniel talking to Bear. "I gave you your food. It's not my fault you inhaled it like a vacuum."

Only silence greeted this statement.

"Don't give me those eyes. You're a very talented manipulator, but I don't cave to those kinds of tactics."

Jessica walked as quietly as she could to the entrance of the kitchen so she could see.

Bear was begging expectantly, and Daniel stood next to the dog food cabinet.

"Fine," he said, rolling his eyes the way he had at her just a few minutes earlier. "You can have one treat. But that's it. Someone has to insist on discipline in this house."

He got a dog treat out of the cabinet and handed it to Bear, who crunched it happily.

Then he reached out to scratch her ears, and the dog nuzzled his hand.

Jessica almost started to cry as she stood watching.

Daniel loved Bear, no matter how he might say differently. There was no way to misread his expression.

She wanted this man so much—with all his kindness and intelligence and humor and strength and stubbornness and brooding depth.

She wanted him all the way.

She wanted to share life with him. To have his children. To grow old with him.

She wanted to love and be loved.

And it hurt so much that she couldn't have all of it. It seemed *wrong* in a way she couldn't articulate.

He'd crouched down to stroke the length of Bear's back, but he straightened quickly when he realized she was present.

"This dog is the most demanding creature I've ever seen." Then he must have processed her expression because he made a rough burst of sound and strode over to her. "Jessica, you have to tell me what's wrong."

She controlled her expression, although it physically hurt her to do so. "It's nothing. I'm just emotional today, I guess."

"Emotional about what?"

She looked away. "Everything."

He started to object, but then must have glanced at the clock. "We've got to go, but we're going to talk about this later tonight. So you might as well resign yourself right now to telling me what's wrong."

At least she had a short reprieve. She could pull herself together and figure out something to tell him later tonight.

She could tell him some of the truth without telling him all of it.

They took her car over to the church since his truck was still getting worked on.

Jessica lit the candles in the displays in the windows of the sanctuary as Daniel got his stuff together and found the Scripture readers so he could be sure they knew what to do.

The service was a traditional lessons and carols service, with a short homily and then "Silent Night" sung as individual candles were lit. It was the same Christmas Eve service she'd attended all her life, and she'd always deeply loved it.

The service was beautiful and grave. The carols and Scripture passages were much loved and familiar. She tried to focus on spiritual issues, the beautiful truth of God becoming human to save them, instead of on her own crushed heart.

She mostly succeeded.

But then, just before Daniel got up to give the homily, she glanced over at him, where he was sitting behind the pulpit.

He was gazing at her, and there was something in his expression that she knew, she recognized, she'd seen in him before, she'd felt in herself. Like he was gazing at something he wanted desperately but knew he could never have.

In that moment, it looked like he loved her.

She saw it—felt it—for a few seconds, but then his face changed, and he glanced away. And it felt like something was taken away from her, something she'd never really had.

Her eyes were burning when he stood up and began to talk about how this one birth, this one life, was the center of everything, transformed everything, remade everything.

She was fighting not to cry as he spoke about how the incarnation was the absolute manifestation of love. And she was strangling on emotion when he concluded that this one truth changes us, gives meaning to lives that would otherwise not have them.

By the time he was done, she couldn't control herself anymore—she was about to break down completely—so she slipped out of the pew and out the side door of the sanctuary as he spoke the prayer before the final hymn.

She stood in the hallway of the church for a moment, paralyzed, with no idea what she should do. Irrationally, it felt like her entire body was cracking with her heart.

With no way to control herself, she headed toward Daniel's office, where she could be alone for a few minutes and pull herself together.

She had her hand on the doorknob when she heard his voice say from behind her, "Jessica."

She paused, motionless, her hand gripping the knob.

The congregation had just started to sing "Silent Night." The sanctuary would be dark, and they'd begin to light their candles now.

"You should get back in there," she said raspingly. "They'll wonder where you went."

"I should be right here." He looked frustrated and concerned and utterly helpless. "You need to tell me what's wrong right now. *Right now.*"

"I don't know if I can do this," she burst out, no defenses anymore, no way to hold the truth back.

His face grew very still. "You can't do what? The marriage?"

She wiped away a couple of tears, hating that she couldn't stop crying. "I don't know if I can do it. I thought I could. I wanted to. But it's not enough. I want *more*. I can't help but want more."

His brow lowered slightly as he stared at her. "What do you want, honey? I'll try to give you anything you need."

She shook her head, even his earnestness hurting her since it was so close to what she wanted from him. But just not all the way there. "I don't think you can." She took a shaky exhale and finally processed the realization she'd had in the service earlier, the one that had changed everything. "That's not right. You *can*. You just *won't*."

"I won't what?"

"You won't let yourself love me."

He froze, the way she'd frozen a minute ago.

It was too late for pride or deflection or any sort of defense, so she let the words spill out. "You could. I know you could. You could love me the way I love you. But you just won't allow yourself to. And I don't know if I can be okay with the half of yourself you're willing to give me."

He swallowed so hard she saw it in his throat. "Jessica, honey—"

"Don't call me 'honey' unless you mean it. You can't have it both ways. I know it's hard. I know how hard it's been for you. I know how you've suffered, and I understand why you're angry about it. Why you can't trust that anything good will last. I understand. I really do. But I don't think I'm okay with this."

He reached for her, something strange happening on his face, but she jerked away from his touch, afraid it would undo her.

"I'm sorry Lila died," she went on, her voice cracking on almost every word. "I'm so sorry it happened. It's horrible. *Horrible.* And nothing is ever going to make her death good. It's proof that something is wrong with the world—that things like that happen. That people like her die. That they're taken away from us. The world is broken. It's just broken."

She sucked in a harsh breath and palmed more tears away. Daniel tried to reply, but she talked over him. "But you're acting like that's the end of the story, that the brokenness is the final answer. When you know very well that it's not. You've always said that at the end of the story the world will be healed, fixed, all wrongs finally righted. And that what's broken is being redeemed, little by little, even now."

"Jessica—"

"I've always believed that, and I thought you believed it too. My mother is dying—"

She broke off, her shoulders shaking, the emotion almost overwhelming.

Daniel reached out for her again, but she shook him away.

"She's dying, little by little, and there's nothing good about that. And I couldn't get up on Christmas morning—on *any* morning—if I thought her deterioration was the last thing, the only thing. If there wasn't real hope that her mind and her body and my heart will be made whole again. You know all this. You *know* it. You know that what God does is make us whole when we're nothing but broken. But you're not acting like you believe it."

She was crying so hard she could barely see Daniel in front of her. She could hear the congregation singing the last stanza of "Silent Night."

"And if you *don't* believe it, then what are we doing here?" She gestured between them to indicate their marriage.

Then she gestured toward the sanctuary. "And if you don't believe it, what are you doing *there*?"

Her eyes cleared enough for her to see his face. He was just staring at her, evidently paralyzed. Trapped. Unable to take the final step.

And she couldn't stand it. Couldn't stand that he simply wouldn't love her.

She whirled around and stumbled away from him, out of the church, down the sidewalk in the cold and blowing snow, and to her car.

She drove home, half-blinded by tears.

Christmas Eve was supposed to be about hope. That had always been the whole point.

So it was ironic—in the bitterest of ways—that this was the night when her hope for her marriage finally died.

# TWELVE

Jessica was still sobbing as she opened the front door and stepped in.

She loved this old house. Even though she'd lived here less than a month, it already felt like home. Like she belonged.

But it also felt like Daniel, so just walking through the entryway made her chest hurt even more. Responding to the pain, without even thinking through the gesture, she grabbed her wedding ring and engagement ring and pulled them off her finger, setting them down on the entry table where she left her keys.

She couldn't wear them anymore.

She crouched down to greet Bear, who nuzzled at her face in concern. When she could summon enough energy, she stood up and trudged upstairs.

Her sobs faded to blurred stupor, she got out a suitcase from the spare bedroom and started to throw clothes into it.

She wasn't even sure why.

It just felt like she needed to get away—get out of here—as soon as she possibly could.

But she had nowhere to go.

She'd given up the little rental house in Charlotte she'd had before. She had no family except her mother. She couldn't stay with anyone in Willow Park—there would be no possible way to explain why she'd left Daniel.

She could go to Kim's in Asheville. Or she could go to a hotel.

Those were the only choices she could come up with.

She sat down on the bed and leaned over, shaking so helplessly she literally couldn't breathe for a minute.

She didn't want to leave.

She loved it here—in Willow Park. Her hometown. Where she wanted to be.

She loved the life she'd started to build here and the way she was starting to connect with other people. It could keep getting better. She could be part of his community.

She loved Daniel, and she couldn't stand the thought of life without him. Other than her mother, he'd been the most important person in her life for long before they'd gotten married.

But now, because she'd wanted too much, she would lose everything.

Bear was lying in a pitiful heap at her feet, completely overwhelmed by Jessica's obvious distress. She stood up just then and poked her nose toward Jessica's face.

She was still leaning forward, her head almost to her knees, so she reached over and stroked the dog's soft fur.

"I know," she said, her voice so hoarse it was almost unrecognizable. "I don't know what to do. I know you love him too, but I think we may need to leave. I don't know what to do."

Bear gazed up at her adoringly, as if hopeful that Jessica's mood was improving.

Or maybe she was just hoping for food.

"But I guess I should wait to talk to him first. Maybe…"

She didn't know if there was a maybe. It didn't feel like there was any hope.

Before Jessica could think through the situation more rationally, before she could even move, the front door to the house opened and then banged shut.

Then she heard loud, fast footsteps on the stairs.

Jessica was too dazed to do anything except look toward the bedroom door.

Daniel burst in, flushed, sweating under his dress shirt, and gasping for air.

Jessica straightened up with a jerk at the sight of him. Her mouth opened in a question she couldn't voice.

His eyes took in Jessica and then the suitcase on the bed. They were strangely wild. She'd never seen that expression before. "Don't leave," he rasped through his panting. "Please, honey... don't leave me."

Baffled and disoriented and flooded with a crashing wave of hope, she gaped at him. "Why are you panting?" she asked stupidly.

"I... ran... home."

Her eyes widened. "Why did you run all the way home?"

"You took..." He was gasping so much now he had to bend over, sucking in loud, urgent breaths. "Took the car."

"Oh." She hadn't even realized she'd stranded Daniel at church without a car since his truck was in the shop.

He looked like he'd run a marathon with his shirt sticking damply to his chest and perspiration dripping from his face despite how cold it was out.

She glanced at the bedside clock and gasped. "How did you get here so quickly?"

"I ran... fast."

He must have sprinted home at a dead run to cover the distance so quickly. She stared at him in awe, trying not to assume this meant what she was hoping it meant. She'd been disappointed before.

"Please don't leave me, Jessica," he gasped, straightening up again. "I know I haven't—"

He had to stop and bend over again to try to breathe.

"Catch your breath first," she said in concern. "I don't want you to have a heart attack."

He nodded and braced himself on the dresser, clearly trying to even out his breathing. Then he threw a quick glance over his shoulder. "Please don't leave... until I can talk."

"I won't leave."

This seemed to satisfy him, and he took a minute to catch his breath, wipe the sweat from his face, and pull himself together.

Jessica tried to be patient. Tried not to shake whatever he wanted to tell her out of him.

She kept imagining her handsome pastor of a husband leaving the Christmas Eve service before it was over and racing through their little town to get home to her.

When he'd managed to recover enough, he turned around and came toward her, sinking onto his knees in front of her.

"Jessica, honey, please don't leave me. I know I haven't treated you right. I know I don't deserve for you to give me a second chance. I know I haven't been the kind of husband I should have been to you. But please don't leave me."

He glanced over at the suitcase again, and Jessica suddenly felt guilty about how her first instinct had been to run away before they'd even talked about it more. She started to say, "I—"

"I love you so much, honey." He took both of her hands in his and gazed up at her with an utterly naked expression of adoration. "I've been an ass... a jerk about everything—trying to hold back my feelings—because I'm so out-of-my-mind crazy about you that it threw my whole world out of alignment. If I admitted it to myself, if I let myself love you for real, then I'd have to admit that all the anger and resentment I was holding onto was futile, was utterly wrong."

Jessica's lips parted, and the roomed spun around her as she tried to process what he was saying.

"You were right," he went on, his voice hoarse and broken. "You were absolutely right about what you said back at the church. I've been stupid and selfish and arrogant, and I've clung to control so much that I pushed away everything I want. I didn't want to give him the chance to take you away from me too. But you're a gift. A gift to me from God. And I've been throwing it back in his face."

She'd been crying just a minute before, so she had no way to control the emotion now. Tears poured down her cheeks.

"Oh, honey, please don't cry. I know I've hurt you. I know I've let you down. But I want to be the husband that you need, that you deserve. I was in love with you long before we ever got married. Did you know that? I've been fighting the feelings for so long, but it's always been a losing battle."

She was shaking now, her hands trembling in his grip.

Daniel wasn't finished yet. "But it was the wrong battle, and I surrender completely. Please give me the chance to show you how much I love you, how much I know what a blessing you are. I want to wake up every Christmas morning and know—and know for sure, absolutely—that everything broken in this world will one day, finally, be made whole. I want to know it for sure because you're in my arms."

This was evidently the end of his outpouring of passionate feeling because he stopped talking and squeezed her hands, but she still couldn't respond. She was so overwhelmed she couldn't stop crying. Not gentle tears but loud, ugly sobbing like before.

"Jessica?" Daniel said, after he'd been silent for a moment and she'd done nothing but cry. "Are you all right?"

She tried to answer but couldn't, so she just nodded her head urgently.

His face twisted as he reached up to cup her face with one hand. "Honey, can you please try to say something? I'm dying here, and I don't know if your crying is a good thing or a bad thing."

"It's a good thing," she managed to choke out. "It's a good thing."

She watched through tears as his face transformed with a relief so visceral she could almost feel it too.

"So you're not going to leave me?" he asked.

She shook her head. "No. No. No. No." She sniffed and gasped and tried to pull herself together.

"So you'll wear your rings again?" he asked, reaching down for her left hand.

She discovered then that he'd seen her rings on the table and picked them up. He'd had them clenched in his hand all this time.

A new wave of emotion overtook her as he slid the rings back on her finger. She nodded like an idiot. Still couldn't say much of anything.

"Do you think you could maybe stop crying?" Despite the deep emotion evident in his expression, a little glint of wry amusement appeared in his eyes.

"I'm trying!" she wailed.

He laughed then and stood up from his knees—but only to sit down on the edge of the bed beside her and pull her into his arms.

She choked some more against his chest, adoring the feel of his arms around her, even though they clutched her so tightly it was almost uncomfortable.

When her sobs finally subsided, she shifted until he released her.

"I love you so much!" she burst out, pleased she'd managed to get something coherent said.

He took her face in both of his hands. "You said that before, but I can't quite believe it. Do you really?"

"Yes, I love you. I love you so much. I've loved you for a really long time."

With a groan, he pulled her into his arms again, but this time the hug only lasted a minute because he pulled away enough to kiss her.

They kissed urgently, clumsily, rather wetly. She clawed at his shoulders and clutched at his hair and couldn't seem to get him close enough, deep enough.

They fell backward onto the bed with her sprawled on top of him as their tongues tangled and his hands slid down to her bottom.

Then a thought suddenly sliced through her emotion-fogged brain. She jerked her mouth away with a gasp. "The church! The service wasn't even over. Did you just run out without telling anyone?"

He'd obviously gotten into the embrace too much for his brain to work with its normal alacrity. He stared up at her, looking rather dazed, and his pelvis rocked up slightly against her weight in a way that was impossible to misinterpret.

"You can't just run out on a Christmas Eve service. You're the pastor!"

"I told Micah," Daniel said at last, the question finally penetrating to his brain. "He was going to give the final benediction."

"What did he say?"

"He said 'finally.'" Daniel looked slightly sheepish. "He's been telling me for months that I need to get it together or I'll lose you. I can't believe I almost proved him right."

For some reason, this made Jessica even giddier—like it was tangible proof that Daniel's feelings for her were real if Micah knew about them too.

"But what will everyone at church think about you running out on the service that way?"

"They'll think I had urgent business to take care of with my wife." He smiled up at her, with a hot, teasing expression she loved. "Which I do."

"Okay. That sounds reasonable."

He grabbed her and pulled her back into a kiss and then rolled them both over. He kissed and stroked and undressed her until she was deeply aroused, and then he settled between her legs and entered her slowly.

She let her breath out with a silly whine of pleasure when he'd sunk fully inside her. She clung to him, all of him, in every way she could.

He'd lowered his face onto her shoulder, breathing heavily, not moving, simply sheathed inside her. She'd never felt so close to another person in her life.

She stroked his back and his shoulders. Slid her hands up into his hair. Felt like she was shuddering inside with more than she could possibly hold.

He finally raised his head, kissed her, and whispered, "You have no idea how much I love you."

Jessica burst into tears again.

Mortified, she wept in frantic little sobs as Daniel held himself tensely above her, staring at her in bewilderment.

"Jessica?" he said at last. "You have to tell me what's wrong."

"Nothing's wrong," she choked, trying desperately to control herself. "Everything's good." Her body was shaking as she cried, and she could feel Daniel's hard length moving inside her with each quivering vibration.

His face strained, Daniel started kissing away her tears and shifted his forearms until his hands were holding the back of her head, tangled in her hair—it was as close as he could get to an embrace in their present position. "If everything was good, you wouldn't be crying."

She shook her head, finally managing to stop the sobs although the tears were still streaming down into her hair.

"I'm happy," she said foolishly, wishing she could better explain how she was feeling. How having everything she'd wanted for so long had simply flooded over in this torrent of emotion.

Apparently he understood enough. He met her gaze deeply, his eyes reflecting a matching blaze of joy and love. But then he managed to say with impressive irony, "Honey, if we don't get it together soon, you'll really have something to cry about. I'd like to last for more than one thrust."

She started to laugh and pulled him down into another wet kiss. Then he started to move. The first few thrusts were slow and deep, and they made her shudder with pleasure. But he couldn't maintain that leisurely pace for long, and he soon accelerated his motion, driving into her faster and harder. After only a minute, he was sweating again beneath his clothes, and something wild had entered his eyes.

She drew up her legs, bending them more at the knee. She clung to his back and rocked her hips up toward him, trying to match his frantic motion.

"It's good." She gasped as she felt jolts of pleasure shoot through her with each stroke inside her. "Daniel, it's so good."

"Yeah." He panted, too far gone to say anything very coherent. He was still cupping her head in his hands, his fingers occasionally fisting in her hair. "Good, Jessica, good."

She had waited so long for this. For this intimacy to be whole, complete, to unquestionably mean love.

She started shaking beneath him more frantically, trying to claim the orgasm that was mounting too slowly. "Daniel," she choked, reaching up in an attempt to hold his face in her hands. "Love this. Love you."

He was moving urgently now, with so much momentum that the bed was knocking against the wall. He muttered a series of words in rhythm with his thrusting. It was mostly under his breath, but she occasionally caught the sound of her name and the word "love."

And it was his love as much as his body that pushed her into climax. She arched in a sudden wave of pleasure, her mouth falling open in a silent cry.

He was right behind her, and he met her eyes as he came inside her, filling her with all that he had.

Jessica, coming down from her own release, almost had to look away from what she saw in his eyes. It was so raw, so naked, so completely vulnerable. So rich, so loving, so close to pure joy.

She couldn't stop herself from crying again. He collapsed on top of her but manage to wrap his arms around her tightly. She sobbed noisily into his shoulder, feeling overwhelmed and blissfully satisfied and absolutely idiotic.

Finally he muttered into her ear dryly, "You keep that up, you're going to give me a complex."

She made a burst of sound that was half laugh and half sob. "I love you, Daniel."

"I love you too." He gave her a teasing grin. "Should I be flattered that my extraordinary talent at sex has reduced you to tears again?"

She laughed again, this time without any crying. "I can't believe I didn't realize how arrogant you were before we got married. Just remember that you didn't have that amazing sex all by yourself. You didn't do it alone."

His grin and mocking expression faded in an instant, and he gazed into her eyes with naked tenderness. "I know that, honey. You have no idea how deeply I know that I could never have done it alone."

She knew he was talking now about so much more than sex, so she got choked up again. This time, however, she managed to maintain her control.

But then he tilted his head until his cheek was pressed against her hair. "Thank you, Jessica."

Her shoulders jerked a little. "Stop," she whimpered, her voice muffled by his skin. "You're going to make me cry again."

"Thank you," he repeated, low and husky, burying his fingers in her hair. "I love you. I love you. I love you."

"Shut up," she demanded desperately, too afraid to even look at him. "No more sweetness. I'm already a puddle of mush. I can't take any more."

He lifted his body off hers just slightly, enough to expose her face. This time he didn't say anything, but his eyes were adoring. She surrendered, sighed, let the tears come, and momentarily reveled in the sappiness.

Life didn't often offer moments of almost perfect bliss, so she might as well enjoy it while it lasted.

It lasted a long time. It lasted until Christmas morning.

∼

The next morning, Jessica woke up feeling blissfully happy.

She knew she was blissfully happy, even before she opened her eyes.

She instinctively rolled over toward Daniel until she realized with a grunt that his side of the bed was empty.

It was then that she opened her eyes.

She sat up abruptly.

The bathroom was empty too.

It was Christmas today, and he'd told her he loved her the night before.

But he'd left her alone again this morning.

Slammed with a surge of outrage, she jumped out of bed and yanked on flannel pants and a sweatshirt.

Bear jumped up from her bed too, evidently believing something exciting was about to happen.

They both ran downstairs and down the hall to the closed door of Daniel's study.

Jessica pounded on it. "Daniel!"

"Don't come in."

"I *will* come in." She tried the doorknob, but it was locked. She pounded on it again. "I know you love me, and I'm not going to believe anything else. You can't hide from me again. If you're upset about something, then you have to tell me what it is!"

Bear snuffled loudly at the crack between the door and the floor as Jessica kept pounding—with the flat of her hand now since her knuckles started to hurt.

She gasped in surprise when the door suddenly swung open.

Daniel was still wearing his pajama pants, although he'd pulled a sweatshirt on as well, and his hair was sticking out in all directions from going to bed last night sweaty.

"I'm not going to let you pull away from me again," she said with all the authority she could muster, trying to push past him into the study since he was blocking her entrance.

He grabbed her and kept her from forcing her way into the room. "I'm not pulling away. Jessica, would you stop pushing. I'm not pulling away."

He was stronger than her, so her attempts to fight his grip were futile. When his words registered, she blinked up at him. "You're not?"

"I'm not."

"Then what are you doing in here with the door locked?"

He gave her a longsuffering look. "I was working on your Christmas presents."

"Oh."

"Yes. Oh."

He was looking far too smug now, so she frowned at him, merely out of principle. "Well, I woke up and you weren't there. And then the study was closed. It happened before, you know, so I thought…"

"I know it happened before." His expression changed. "I'm so sorry it happened before, honey. It's not going to happen again."

"It's not?"

"It's not." He leaned forward to kiss her, but she ducked her head.

He frowned. "I said I wasn't pulling away. Why aren't I allowed to kiss my wife?"

"I haven't brushed my teeth yet."

He chuckled and pulled her into a hug. "Well, go brush your teeth while I finish your presents because I'm definitely going to want to kiss you later."

"Presents? You got me more than one?" She tried to peer past his shoulder into the study. He couldn't have hauled the desk into the study this morning all by himself.

His strong arms stymied her attempts. "No peeking."

She huffed, mostly for show, and let him close the study door again. Then she went to brush her teeth, make coffee, and drag the present she'd bought him down the stairs and into the living room to put under the tree—which was no small feat.

Then feeling so happy she was almost trembling with it, she poured her energy into trying a scratch recipe for cinnamon buns she'd found last week—one that didn't take forever to make or look too difficult for her to manage.

She drank coffee and sang Christmas carols and mixed up her dough and rolled it out until Daniel finally emerged from the study, carrying an armful of presents.

"Oh," she gasped, running over to inspect them. "How many did you get me?"

He turned his body to keep the presents away from her hands. "They're not all for you, so don't get too excited."

"They're not? Who else did you get presents to open for today?" She managed to catch a glimpse of the tag on one of the presents. "You got a present for Bear?"

She was so astonished and delighted at this fact that her voice squeaked.

Daniel attempted to look dignified, which was a challenge lugging an awkward stack of presents and with his hair sticking up straight on end. "You will find out about the presents at the appropriate time."

She giggled and returned to her cinnamon rolls, wanting to hug herself.

He would have had to buy the presents before this morning, which meant even before last night he'd gotten a present for Bear.

She got the rolls in the oven and was heading for the living room when she saw Daniel emerge from the study carrying one last enormous gift.

"Oh, that's a huge one! What is it?"

"Mind your own business."

"It *is* my business. Isn't that my present?"

"No. This one isn't for you."

"Oh. Is it for Bear?" She twisted her head to try to read the tag.

"I've never seen a nosier woman. Can't a man put presents under the tree in peace?"

"Of course not. Can we open them now, or do we have to wait until after breakfast?"

He set the big present under the tree and then turned back to her. His face softened when his eyes rested on her face. "We can do anything you want."

She clapped her hands, too giddy to contain it. "Let's open presents now. But I have to warn you, I only got you one present."

"Well, that works out well since I like giving presents more than getting them."

"It's a really good present though."

"It better be."

"You can open yours last. Bear wants to open hers first."

Bear was snooting around the wrapped gifts, pushing a couple aside until she could snatch one that was in the shape of a bone.

She held the wrapped present in her mouth with obvious satisfaction and wagged her tail, expecting praise for her accomplishment.

Jessica unwrapped the bone with some help from Bear, who kept nosing at the paper, and then the dog settled down to happily chew her big bone.

Then Jessica got to open her presents. Despite Daniel's protests, most of them were for her. He'd gotten her a pair of gorgeous earrings that were way too expensive, cozy fleece pajamas with big white dogs wearing Santa hats on them, a hardback novel about hijinks in a church choir, a beginner's cookbook for people who could barely boil water, and a set of computer-printed "coupons" for free car repair, performed by Daniel, of course.

Jessica was laughing so hard she was almost in tears as she opened the coupon set.

"You've got two more to open," Daniel said, looking adorably pleased with the reception of all his gifts.

She knew one of them was the desk out in the workshop, so she looked at the large wrapped present under the tree. "The big one?"

"No, not the big one." He got up to grab a small box she hadn't noticed behind the larger one.

Jessica immediately unwrapped the box and then lifted the top. Inside was a folded sheet of paper.

Frowning in confusion, she unfolded the paper and stared at it for a minute before the words registered in her mind.

It was a trip itinerary. For a trip to St. Lucia in March.

She blinked a few times and then lifted her eyes to Daniel's face.

He looked just slightly diffident. "I thought maybe we could have a honeymoon. But if you'd rather go somewhere else—"

"No," she cried, throwing herself at him. "It's perfect!"

He laughed, obviously unable to doubt her response was utterly sincere.

"But can we afford it?" she asked, reason returning to her once her excitement had settled slightly.

"Yes, we can afford it."

"Because I don't need an expensive—"

"I said we can afford it." He gave her a stern look. "I'll let you inspect the budget for it, if you must, although it's a gift so you're not supposed to ask about the price."

She hid a smile. "Okay. Just checking." She leaned over to kiss him. "For a rather infuriating man, you really might be the best husband in the world."

"I'm glad you recognize it."

"Now what about my other present?" There was still the large unwrapped gift on the floor, and she had the sudden anxiety that the beautiful desk hadn't been for her after all.

But it had to have been for her. It had three platforms for three computer monitors.

"You can't have your other present. I have to wait until Micah can get over here to help me bring it in."

She let out a sigh of relief at this affirmation. "Can't we just go out and look at it?"

Daniel narrowed his eyes. "You know! You went around peeking and found it in the workshop."

"I didn't mean to peek," she admitted. "I accidentally stumbled on it Sunday morning. It's the most beautiful desk

I've ever seen. I had no idea you could make something like that."

Leaning back against the couch, he smiled over at her. "I've never made anything so hard before. You have no idea how long I worked on that thing. But I had to channel all my feelings for you into something, and the desk was the only thing I allowed myself to do."

She smiled back at him sappily. "It means so much to me that you made it."

They kissed for a minute until Bear set down the remains of her bone to come investigate her owners' inexplicable distraction.

Jessica pulled out of the kiss and stroked the dog's head. "Now what about the big present?"

"I told you that one isn't for you."

"Who is it for?" Jessica got up to look for herself, and Bear came with her.

The dog figured it out before Jessica could inspect the tag.

Bear stepped onto the present and started scratching it up enthusiastically.

"Hey," Jessica said, trying to get the dog off. "You're going to mess it up."

"She's not going to mess it up," Daniel admitted resignedly.

Jessica pulled away the torn wrapping paper to discover the present was a huge, luxury dog bed.

Delighted, Bear turned several circles on it, scratching up a good place to flop down on it.

Jessica was laughing hysterically as she went to give Daniel a hug. "I knew you secretly liked my dog."

"I don't like your dog."

"Yes, you do. Don't try to deny it."

"I don't like her."

"You're a preacher. You shouldn't lie."

"I'm not lying." They were on the couch again, and he settled her more comfortably against him. Their lips were just a breath apart. "I don't like her. I *love* her. But not nearly as much as I love you."

They kissed for a minute, sweetly, gently. Then she said against his lips, "I love you too. Thank you for all my presents."

"You're welcome. I still haven't gotten to open *my* present."

"Oh, yeah. I forgot."

She had gotten him the complete works of Bonhoeffer in a very expensive, beautifully bound hardbacks. They'd been way too expensive, but she knew he'd love them.

"My present can wait." He kissed her again, more deeply this time. "Other things take priority."

"Okay." She kissed him back, and it wasn't long until they were both passionate and excited, Daniel leaning back against the armrest and Jessica on top of him, straddling his hips.

He'd just slipped his hands under her sweatshirt when Jessica became aware of a strong scent penetrating her consciousness.

"What's that?" she asked, pulling up and sniffing the air.

"What do you think it is?" He sounded just a little grumpy at the interruption of their embrace. "It's what happens when your gorgeous body is all on top of me like this."

She choked on a laugh, but was too distracted to follow through on what he'd started to press up against her.

Then the scent finally triggered something in her brain.

"The cinnamon rolls!" she gasped, scrambling up off him and then off the couch and running frantically for the kitchen.

It was without doubt the best Christmas morning she'd had in her life, and she had nothing in the world to complain about.

Except for the fact that the cinnamon rolls were hopelessly burnt.

# ABOUT NOELLE ADAMS

Noelle handwrote her first romance novel in a spiral-bound notebook when she was twelve, and she hasn't stopped writing since. She has lived in eight different states and currently resides in Virginia, where she writes full time, reads any book she can get her hands on, and offers tribute to a very spoiled cocker spaniel.

She loves travel, art, history, and ice cream. After spending far too many years of her life in graduate school, she has decided to reorient her priorities and focus on writing contemporary romances. For more information, please check out her website: noelle-adams.com.

Books by Noelle Adams

*Beaufort Brides Series*
- Hired Bride
- Substitute Bride
- Accidental Bride

*One Night Novellas*

One Hot Night: Three Contemporary Romance Novellas

    One Night with her Boss

    One Night with her Roommate

    One Night with the Best Man

*Willow Park Series*

    Married for Christmas

    A Baby for Easter

    A Family for Christmas

    Reconciled for Easter

    Home for Christmas

*Heirs of Damon Series*

    Seducing the Enemy

    Playing the Playboy

    Engaging the Boss

    Stripping the Billionaire

*Standalones*

    A Negotiated Marriage

    Listed

    Bittersweet

Missing

Revival

Holiday Heat

Salvation

Excavated

Overexposed

Road Tripping

*The Protectors Series (co-written with Samantha Chase)*

Duty Bound

Honor Bound

Forever Bound

Home Bound

Made in the USA
Charleston, SC
03 August 2016